Her So Called
HUSBAND

Her So Called HUSBAND

CHENELL PARKER

Chapter 1
ALEXUS

"Ahhhh!" I screamed loudly as my hair felt like it was being pulled from my scalp through the driver's side window of the car.

I had just pulled up to the gas station about a minute ago before someone reached through the window and was trying to pull me out of it.

Dre had just walked into the store to pay for our gas. I was hoping he would look out of the store's window to see what was happening and intervene. My heart was beating a mile a minute. Not because I was scared, but because it all happened so fast that I didn't have time to react or even see who was behind the attack.

This last year has been the worst year of my life. I've been in so many fights that I've lost count. Tired was not even the word to describe my feelings. I was trying to twist my body at an angle so I could look out of the corner of my eye to see who was giving me the headache of my life when I spotted Dre sprinting our way.

"The fuck is you doing?" he yelled as I felt the death grip on my hair release.

I immediately pulled my hair back in place and hopped out of the car only to come face to face with his wife yet again. To say I was pissed was an understatement. This was the second run in she and I had this week. She somehow shows up everywhere I go even if I'm not with her so-called husband.

She was screaming in Dre's face. "You always claim you not fucking her, but y'all are together every time I roll up on you!"

"Man, go home and stop making a fool of yourself out here in front of all these people. You must want somebody to call the law on ya ass or something," Dre said.

Until he said that, I hadn't noticed that a crowd of people had formed to watch the free show that we were giving. I was still feeling some kind of way about that bitch pulling my hair so I was ready for whatever. At only twenty-one years old, I never imagined that my life would hold this much drama.

Before I met D'Andre Mack two years ago, I was a carefree nineteen year old who worried about nothing but going to college. My best friend, Jada, and I went to our friend Keanna's graduation party and that's when I met Dre, Keanna's first cousin. We clicked immediately and spent a lot of time together. He even took me to Miami for my twentieth birthday.

Imagine my surprise when, eight months into the relationship, I found out that he not only had a girl, but was actually married with four kids! I knew he had someone, but I never thought he was married. He spent nights at my house and we went away for days at a time. He would sometimes leave out of the room to talk on his phone so I knew somebody was in the picture.

I was so hurt that he kept it from me, but I was even more hurt to know that Keanna didn't feel the need to tell me either. She gave me some lame ass excuse about it not being her business, yet she was the one that introduced us.

I tried staying away from Dre and I succeeded for almost a month. The fact that he called me all day apologizing didn't help me get over him either. I had almost been with him for a year by then. My feelings were involved and I was in deeper than I wanted to be. I gave in and continued to be his side chick. I hated that term, but that's exactly what I was. I knew that I could probably have any man I wanted, but I chose to stay with somebody else's husband. I had so much going for myself and any man would be proud to call me his own.

I'm five-four and a hundred and thirty pounds. I had a bad ass shape and a pretty face to match. I was in my second semester of college studying to become a Physical Therapist Assistant. I wasn't shy, but I didn't get around as much as most girls my age.

Before him, I had only been with one other person sexually and that was my ex-boyfriend Malik. I was in love and I didn't know if I would ever come down from this high Dre had me on. My siblings and my mom hated him, but it wasn't enough to tear me away from him.

Dre made me a priority. He spent as much time with me as he spent with his wife and sometimes more. I didn't expect anyone to understand, but I was grown and made my own decisions.

"Since when you did you start letting this bitch drive your car, Dee?" Cherika yelled, snapping me back to the present.

I was ready to go to war with her ghetto ass so I had to say something. "That's the last bitch I'm gon' be tonight. Be mad with the nigga you married to," I said.

That was all her ghetto ass needed to hear. She ran full force at me, but this time I was prepared. I jumped back as she attempted to hit me in the face and countered with a punch that landed on the side of her face. She went crazy and we went into an all-out catfight.

I took all of my anger and aggravation out on her and quickly got the best of her in the fight. For every lick she threw, I threw two more. I was tired of doing this shit. It was getting old. Dre tried pulling us apart to no avail. then he picked his wife up which gave me the opportunity to get a hard lick to her face that split her lip and had blood pouring from it like water.

"Really Dre? How you grab me and let your bitch keep hitting me?" she cried.

"Man chill. Somebody probably already called the police. Get in the car, Lex!" Dre yelled to me.

I refused to move. I wanted to make sure he didn't let that ho go and she tried to swing again.

"Alexus, please just get in the car!" Dre yelled again.

I decided to listen this time. I knew when he said my full name like that he was pissed.

"She's not getting in that car. Let that bitch find a ride. You really doing me like this, Dee? Really? Is that bitch that important to you? Is she more important than me and your kids?" Cherika cried.

I got in the car and rolled the window halfway up so we wouldn't have a repeat of what happened earlier. I also wanted to hear what lie he was going to come up with this time. I listened as she cried and he tried to explain his way out of everything.

"It's not even like that, Cherika. I'm not trying to leave that girl out here so you can call your people to get at her. That's not happening," Dre said.

Did he just call me that girl, I said to myself. I know this nigga is not trying to play me. I continued to listen and thinking about what I wanted to tell him when he got back in the car. I'm done. I refuse to keep fighting over something that isn't rightfully mine to begin with. She was going to get her happy home and I was determined to help her get it by leaving his ass alone.

"Just let me bring her home and we can talk when I get back," Dre said.

"No. You haven't been home in two days Dee. You think I believe that shit? Let me follow you then. I won't get out the car. I just want to make sure you telling the truth this time," she said.

This bitch must really be crazy if she thinks she's going anywhere near my house. I couldn't wait to hear his reply.

"What? I'm not taking you to that girl's house. You buggin' for real," he said.

I swear if he called me that girl one more time I was getting out of this damn car. This time I was getting out to fight his ass and not his wife.

"I already know where the bitch live and I know that's where you been for the last two days. I'm not stupid so stop telling me you're not fucking her when I know you are. Everybody know you're fucking her so just tell the truth! You keep getting caught with the same chick, Dre."

"Man, I'm about to bounce. I'm not doing this with you right now. I'll see you at home in a few," Dre said.

I had the door locked so I reached over and opened the passenger side door for him since I was still in the driver's seat. As soon as Dre let her go, she ran to my side of the car and tried to open the door. Once she realized the door was locked, she became enraged and starting kicking the door and screaming. Dre hopped in on the passenger side just as she stuck her hand in through the partially opened window. This time I was prepared so I moved away so she couldn't grab my hair again.

"Cherika, chill. Damn! You always want some drama. I'm not trying to go jail for no bullshit!" Dre yelled.

Either she didn't hear him or she didn't care **as** she continued to try and grab at me.

"Pull off, Alexus," Dre said.

"What!" I yelled surprised at what he had just told me to do. I couldn't believe what he wanted me to do to his own wife. "I can't do that with her hand halfway through the window."

"I told her stupid ass to chill and go home so that's on her. She'll let go once the car starts moving. Pull off!" he yelled again.

Reluctantly, I put the car in drive and proceeded to slowly pull away hoping that she would take the hint and move away from the car. Unfortunately, this only pissed her off more and she started banging on the glass trying to break it. At Dre's urging, I increased the speed slightly dragging his wife along in the process. Just as I was about to stop in a panic, she let go giving me the green light to press harder on the gas.

I looked over at Dre as he continued to play on his phone like he didn't have a care in the world. I began to question myself and this entire relationship. How can I be so in love with a man who treats his own wife the way he does? When would he start to treat me the same way? This was starting to be too much for me. Now is as good a time as any to let him know how I feel.

"I can't do this anymore," I stated calmly.

It kind of upset me when he kept playing with the phone and didn't reply. I know he was trying to ignore me so I kept talking, hoping to piss him off just as much as I was.

"I'm tired of fighting with your wife and her family every week. I'm sick of her following us every time we go somewhere. And I'm damn sure tired of sharing a man when I know I can get one of my own. You want us both, but yet you want me to be with only you. There are too many niggas out here trying to get at me, but I keep being faithful to a nigga that already got a wife. I think I need to take some of them up on their offers to wife me," I rambled.

I knew this would get his attention. He stopped playing on his phone and told me to pull into another gas station that we were approaching.

We weren't able to get gas at the previous station because his crazy ass wife showed up. This time we both exited the car to pay for the gas to make sure nothing else happened.

Once Dre paid for the gas, we walked back to the car as he informed me that he would drive the rest of the way. I happily handed over his keys, slid in the seat, and slammed the passenger door. He got into the car when he was done, but he didn't move or speak. I could feel him staring at me, but I refused to acknowledge it. I was nervous, but I would never show it.

Before I could say anything, Dre grabbed me by my collar forcing me closer to him as he stared at me through anger-filled eyes.

"If you ever threaten me with a nigga again, I promise you won't like what I'll do to you. Try it and watch you and that nigga get buried. You got me fucked up," Dre said through clenched teeth.

He stared at me a while longer before releasing my shirt and speeding off from the station. I could see the veins popping out of his forehead so I knew he was really mad. Silent tears crept down my face. I knew he would make good on his promise if it ever came down to it. My fear of him is what stopped me from being with someone else.

Dre had a reputation for making his enemies disappear. At only twenty-six years old, he was known to have an extensive record. He had been to jail several times, but never for murder. That alone let me know that he knew what he was doing and he knew how to do it well. The police could never arrest him for selling drugs because he never touched it. His cousin Keanna told me they always got him on some conspiracy or racketeering charges.

He swore that he gave up the drug game, but I doubt he makes the kind of money that he does just by owning two barbershops and two beauty salons. I also know that he owns the house that he and his wife share and he recently purchased a newly built condo in a very prominent area of uptown New Orleans for us. We would usually rent a room when we wanted to chill, but Dre wanted us to have a place of our own. He wanted us to be able to come and go as we pleased and he wanted a place to keep clothes and personal things.

I never stay there alone. If doesn't come through, my best friend Jada and I would sleep there or I would go to one of my brothers' or sisters' houses. I wondered if this was the place that his wife claimed to know about. I wasn't sure, but I would definitely have to be more careful.

"Baby you hear me?" Dre said snapping me from my thoughts.

"Oh so now I'm baby?" I said. "I was that girl when you were talking to your wife a minute ago."

I was fuming mad and I needed to get away from this nigga before I said something else that I would regret.

"I'm not going to the condo. Take me to my sister's house," I told him.

I wasn't trying to give up no ass to him and I knew that's what would have happened if I went to our spot.

"That's what you mad about?" he had the nerve to ask me.

Was this nigga serious? Just a minute ago, he was threatening me, but I didn't bring that back up.

"No. I'm not mad about nothing. I promised my sister that I would watch her kids for her," I lied.

"Yeah alright," he replied.

I didn't care if he knew I was lying or not. I just wanted to be by myself. I needed to talk to my bestie and cry on her shoulder for a while.

I sent Jada a text just as Dre was pulling up to my sister's apartment. I tried to hurry out of the car, but he stopped me.

"I'm sorry for what happened with Cherika and for grabbing you like I did. I meant what I said, but I shouldn't have ruffed you up like that."

I was still upset, but his apology softened me up a little. Dre got out of the car and came around to open my door for me. Once I got out, he pulled me into him and whispered, "I love you Lex," as he held onto me. I didn't respond, but the feeling was definitely mutual.

Dre and I walked to my sister's door hand and hand.

"I'm giving you your space tonight since I know you feeling some kind of way about everything that happened, but we're staying at the spot tomorrow."

Before I could answer my sister, Ayanna, snatched the front door open to see who was outside. She couldn't stand Dre so she frowned up and rolled her eyes once she saw that it was him. When Ayanna closed the door, Dre and I hugged for a while before I pulled away to go inside. He pulled me back and stuck his tongue into my mouth forcing me to open my mouth for him. When I pulled away this time, I hurried through the front door before I changed my mind and left with him anyway. My sister looked at me and rolled her eyes before speaking.

"I don't know why you don't leave his dog ass alone. He ain't never leaving his wife."

I didn't even respond. I was used to her hating on Dre and I really thought she was jealous. She had three kids by three different men and none of them stayed with her for more than six months. They didn't even take care of their kids. I was determined to be the opposite of what she was. She talked all that shit, but the money I got from Dre helped her kids stay fresh because she damn sure couldn't afford to do it workingpart time at Target.

This was the reason I never told her anything. She was too negative. I walked down the hall to my niece's room and plopped down on the floor to call Jada to come and get me. I wasn't in the mood for my sister's bitching so I was giving her my ass to kiss just as soon as my ride pulled up.

Chapter 2
D'ANDRE

I know Lex was lying when she said she had to babysit, but I didn't push the issue like I usually do. I know my baby girl was mad, but I swear I didn't know Cherika's crazy ass was following me. She must have followed me to our spot when I went to pick Alexus up earlier. It didn't matter if she knew where it was. The security was tight and she would never find our condo unless somebody showed her exactly where it was. All of the properties looked the same and it was hard to tell one from the other.

She had to be following us for a while before she made her move. We had been to the movies and out to eat before we even stopped at the gas station. Why did she wait so long to confront us? That didn't make much sense to me.

Cherika and I had been married for six years, but we had been together for eight. We've known each other all our lives, but we decided to take it a step further when I was eighteen and she was twenty-one. Now I'm twenty-six, she's twenty-nine, and we have four kids together. Well at least I think we do. Baby number four was in question. She claimed to be so faithful when I was locked up, but Keanna put me down on some of the foul shit she did.

Cherika was the type of chick that was down for whatever especially when it came to me. I was in and out of jail for most of our relationship and she held me down each and every time, but whenever I got out, I did the same stupid shit. I cheated on her every time I had the chance. She always took me back and held me down. That was until I went back for a probation violation the last time. I was given six months and I just knew she wasn't going anywhere during that short period of time, but I was dead wrong.

For the first month, she didn't come see me and she refused to put anything on my books. I had to call everybody in her family just to try and talk to her. I had finally convinced her to come see me and she laid it all out on the table for me. She said she was done unless I put a ring on it. I couldn't believe she had given me an ultimatum. I just knew her hating ass sisters had got in her head. We had never even talked about marriage before then.

I couldn't depend on my family since they all depended on me to take care of them. I was stuck and the only way out was to do the marriage thing, which we ended up doing from behind bars a month later. Just like that, Cherika was back to her old self again. She kept my books full and never missed a visit. The only problem was that marriage didn't mean as much to me as it meant to her. I was still the same D-Mack I was before I married her. I still kept a bitch or two on the side and I came and went as I pleased. I always got caught with my pants down, but it never stopped me. I would give up whoever I got caught with and play the role of the good husband for a while until I met somebody else that I just had to slide up in. This was the first time I fucked around and fell in love with one of my sidepieces.

I don't know what it was about Alexus that had me gone. I lost count of the many broads I cheated on Cherika with, but this was different and she knew it. That was the thing that she couldn't take. She never had to worry about me catching feelings and she knew I would always come home. She hated Alexus and she made sure that everybody knew it. It killed her that Alexus was much younger than she was and she couldn't deny that my baby girl was indeed a bad bitch.

Don't get me wrong, Cherika was pretty and her body was alright, but after four kids and a lifetime in the streets, she couldn't compete with Alexus at all. She had a gut and I couldn't tell if it was from having four kids or all the beer she drank. She was ignorant as hell with a loud foul mouth. Working was out of the question, but the club was mandatory. I tried to encourage her to go back to school and get a degree, but that wasn't happening. The money wasn't an issue since I could afford to pay for whatever she needed for her education.

That was one of the things I loved about Alexus. She didn't play about her education. She refused to miss school and she studied all the time. Even if we were at our spot, she would go in her study area that I made for her and stay locked up for hours at a time. I knew not to bother her and she would ignore me if I did. She was determined to be better than her sisters and mom. They all worked just to get by and she wanted more for herself. I was determined to make sure she got any and everything she wanted, even if I lost my wife in the process.

I rode around for a while smoking and thinking. I wasn't ready to go home yet especially since I knew Cherika would be bitching all night. I was hoping that she would have calmed down by the time I got home. I know I was wrong for telling baby girl to pull off on her, but she knows I don't do the police and I was sure somebody had called them. I was on probation for the next two and a half years and I wasn't trying to go back to jail for her and nobody else.

I ended up going to a hole in the wall bar called Pee-Wee's in Marrero to see if Eric was around. This was his spot and he never missed a weekend here. As soon as I pulled up, I saw a gang of niggas hanging outside and my brother was in the mix. I stepped out of my CLS 500 and walked over to the group.

"What's up with y'all? I know y'all broke asses ain't gambling." I joked. My brother was known to be a jokester so he always had a slick answer.

"Yeah," Eric said, "I'm trying to help this nigga here buy some teeth."

He was cracking on his homeboy who lost his three front teeth in a fight a few months back. Everybody fell out laughing and I joined in. I noticed Keanna's boyfriend Troy standing there with a foul expression on his face.

Back in the day, Troy and I were tight. Right before I went back to jail the last time, he started acting shady for some reason. He always seemed to be on some hating type shit. He used to get his work from me and I would always look out for him, but I couldn't trust him any more so I stopped doing business with him. Nobody wanted to deal with him because he always fucked up their money. It looked like the nigga was getting high judging by the amount of weight he was losing. He sold a little weed here and there, but he wasn't seeing major money like when he fucked with me.

Keanna couldn't see the changes in the nigga, but everybody else did. He didn't even take pride in his appearance any more. For some reason it seemed like he had a problem with me more than anybody else. He always had a boot in his mouth when he looked at me. I really didn't give a fuck, but I made sure to keep my eyes on that nigga at all times.

"What's up Troy?" I hollered at the nigga despite him mean mugging me. I knew that was only pissing him off even more.

"Ain't shit up," he replied with an attitude. That only made me want to fuck with him more. "Let me get in on the next game. I got a few stacks to blow. My baby girl want go shopping anyway. I might as well let you niggas foot the bill!" I yelled. I guess that nigga really did feel some kind of way cause he dapped a few dudes up and went back in the bar.

"What's up with that nigga?"

"Man I don't know, but I don't trust his ass. He was alright until you pulled up. I guess he's still salty 'cause you don't front him anymore," my brother answered.

That was exactly the reason why I stopped. Something was up with that nigga and I wasn't trying to figure out what it was. Just as I was about to tell my brother my feelings, Cherika called me. I stepped away from the crowd to talk, but I was so loud they still heard me. She was yelling about what time I was coming home like she usually did. I hung up on her and went back to where my brother was standing.

"Nigga, Cherika gon' kill yo' stupid ass. Keep playing if you want to. You know she's crazy," my brother joked.

"Man ain't nobody thinking about Cherika stupid ass. She showed her ass earlier."

I told my brother everything that happened at the gas station today. He and everybody else thought it was funny as hell. My brother and I were very close so he knew everything. He really liked Alexus, but there were very few people that Eric didn't like. My entire family knew about Alexus. Even my pops who was on his way home from doing a five-year prison bid wanted to meet her since I talked about her so much. My moms and my sisters didn't like her because they were team Cherika. My brother didn't care one way or the other so he was the only one who welcomed my baby girl into the family.

I hung out with my brother and his friends for a few more hours before I decided to head home. I tried calling my baby before I turned in for the night, but after three back-to-back calls, she still didn't answer. All kinds of crazy thoughts were running through my head and none of them were good. I know I was selfish. I just couldn't picture Alexus with nobody else. I knew she had sex with her ex-boyfriend, but I wasn't worried about that. He was long gone. I hoped like hell she wasn't trying to play games with me because my heart couldn't take it. After trying again for the fourth time, I decided to leave her a message.

"Man, I know you see me blowing your phone up. I don't know what kind of games you're playing, but you better call me back. Don't make me come to your sister's house this time of the night."

I hung up the phone and decided to go home and get this shit over with. It was almost one in the morning and I knew her ass was up waiting for me.

When I pulled up to my driveway I thought the weed and the liquor had me seeing things. I just knew she didn't have her messy ass sisters in my house this late. I hopped out the car ready to curse all those hoes out, but they must have seen when I pulled up. The front door opened and out came Thing 1 and Thing 2 followed by Cherika. Those are the names I gave her two messy ass sisters, Cherice and Charde.

They looked me up and down as they exited my house. I dared one of them bitches to say one word to me. They didn't like me and it was no secret that I couldn't stand their asses either. I walked through the front door and the house looked a mess as usual.

Cherika was lazy as hell. I wasn't a nasty nigga and that drove me crazy. There were plenty of times when I paid my moms and my aunt to come get the house in order for me while she laid around smoking and drinking. I swear if she asked for a divorce I would sign the papers right now. I knew that would never happen, but I wouldn't be hurt if it did. I couldn't bring myself to ask for a divorce especially since she was the only one holding me down for all these years.

She did things that risked her freedom and could have possibly gotten her killed. I knew I would be forever indebted to her, but I didn't want to be married to her forever. I would definitely make sure that she and my kids were always taken care of no matter what, but I needed a way out of this marriage.

As soon as she came back in the house, she started going off.

"I'm tired of you putting that young bitch before me. I have been through everything with you Dee. All I ask if for you to be is faithful, but you can't even do that. You bringing her around your family like you married to her. You know your mama and your sisters tell me everything, but I guess you don't care about that. And now you got her driving your car too. That's just disrespectful." She yelled.

"Man, you want talk about disrespect, but how you got your bum ass sisters in my house smoking and drinking while my kids are here? And then this damn house looks like a fuckin' mess. You always throwing in my face the fact that you my wife, but you don't act like one. You don't cook. You never clean up. All you do is shop, smoke, and drink. That shit is unattractive."

"It's unattractive, but you smoke and drink too. So it's cool for you to do it and not me?"

I couldn't believe this broad. She missed the whole point.

"That's different. You supposed to be a wife and a mother. You need to go back to school or do something with yourself. Get a job or something."

I was getting aggravated with this conversation. And the fact that I still hadn't heard from Alexus only made the shit worse. I was just about to finish going in on Cherika when my phone started ringing and I saw my baby girl picture pop up on the screen. I know I shouldn't have answered the phone, but I couldn't help myself. I needed to know what was up with her. I rushed out of the living room to the bathroom upstairs in the hall with Cherika hot on my heels.

"I know you're not rushing off to answer the phone for that bitch!" she screamed. I closed and locked the door before she had a chance to slip in there with me. I tried whispering so she wouldn't hear what I was saying.

"Where the fuck you at?" I whispered.

"I'm at Jada's house," she said pissing me off. It sounded like she was asleep, but I didn't care. I dropped her off at her sister's house so I don't understand how she ended up at her friend's house.

Cherika was kicking the door and screaming for me to open it up, but my mind was on Alexus. I just knew she was up to something.

"What is all that noise?" she asked.

"Don't worry about that. Why are you at Jada's house when I dropped you off at your sister's? How did you get there?"

She paused and that drove me crazy. I just knew she was trying to come up with a lie to tell. I didn't even give her a chance to answer before I went off.

"You know what? Don't even answer that cause you gon' lie anyway with your sneaky ass. I'll deal with you tomorrow." I said as I hung up. I was heated, but I couldn't do shit about it tonight. I had other problems to deal with. One of which was trying to break down the bathroom door at the moment. Man my life was all fucked up right now, but I was determined to get everything back on track.

As soon as I opened the door, Cherika rushed me trying to take my phone out of my hand. I know

She was dying to get a number on Alexus, but that wasn't happening again. My baby got her number changed five times over the last two years because she kept getting a hold of it and playing on her phone. I pushed her back as she tried to swing on me. I didn't like putting my hands on females, but I really think she liked the shit.

"Cherika, go head man. Stop putting your hands on me before I hit you back." I tried to be calm and walk away, but she just kept following me trying to swing.

"Nigga, I wish you would hit me behind that bitch. I'm sick of this," she cried.

I was sick of it too. If she would divorce me, we could probably both be happy. But I know that was wishful thinking. I went to my kids' room to make sure they were still sleeping since she was screaming and hollering like it was daytime. I hated that they were put in the middle of all of our madness, but there was only so much that I could do.

Once I made sure they were straight, I went down the hall to our room ignoring my wife the entire time. I know this drove her crazy, but

I wasn't in the mood to argue. I just wanted to get some rest. I planned on getting up early to see what the deal was with Alexus. She was going to be on my mind all night. I really needed to spend some time with my kids. I always made plans to do something with them, but something always came up. They were at my mom's house most of the time because Cherika and I were always on the go.

I felt a stinging pain in the back of my head breaking me out of my thoughts. That crazy bitch slapped the hell out of me. Everything in me went numb as I turned around and wrapped my hands around her neck trying to choke the life out of her. She tried to pry my hand away, but my grip was too strong. I saw her gasping for air as her eyes watered and pleaded for me to let her go. I dropped her to the floor and she sucked in a mouthful of air trying to regulate her breathing.

I grabbed my keys and sprinted down the stairs and out the front door. It was a little after two o'clock in the morning, but I didn't care. I called Alexus and told her that I was on my way to pick her up. She could go back to sleep when we got to our spot. I had so much on my mind and I just needed to be around her right now. Cherika really made me step outside of my usually calm character. One thing was for sure, if I didn't realize it before I damn sure knew it now. This marriage was definitely over.

Chapter 3
CHERIKA

As soon as I heard the front door slam, I knew that Dre was gone. I couldn't believe he choked me out like that and just left. He didn't even stay to make sure I was alright. I went to our master bathroom to look at myself in the mirror. My eyes were red and swollen and my neck was bruised from where Dre had choked me. I stared at my reflection in the mirror and just cried. That seemed to be all I did lately. My marriage seemed to be falling apart.

I loved Dre more than life itself. He wasn't perfect and I knew that before I married him, but I was never giving up on my husband or my marriage. I didn't care what my family or anyone else had to say. It was definitely till death do us part. I had Dre's back no matter what. When he was in and out of jail, I was there every step of the way. My sisters convinced me to give him an ultimatum when he went back the last time. Either he married me or I was done. My sisters felt that with all the bullshit he put me through the least he could do was make us official and they were right.

I was skeptical at first but I was happy that everything worked out and Dre made me his wife. I know some people were saying that I forced him into marriage but I didn't give a damn. I had my man and I was happy. I just prayed that he came to his senses before it was too late because divorce was out of the question for me. I know a lot of bitches wished they were in my shoes.

Dre was one of the finest men on the west bank of New Orleans. He's 6'1 with a perfect caramel complexion and a perfect body to match. He had no flaws as far as I could see and I was the only woman lucky enough to have his last name. I earned the ring on my finger and so much more.

I can't count the number of fights I got into over my husband. At the end of the day, he still came home with me. Well he used to. Ever since Alexus came into the picture, everything changed. I never knew if my husband was coming home or not. He used to make excuses for his absences in the beginning, but after a while that stopped too. Everybody knew about Dre's side chick. His entire family had met her but I was the wife so she was never accepted.

Dre's sisters and his mom all loved me. They refused to deal with another woman. His brother Eric was another story. He was in her company just as much as Dre was and I couldn't stand him for it. Dre's cousin, Keanna, and I were very close. I knew that she was friends with Alexus because they went to the same high school. Me and Keanna's relationship was different because we were family. She was Dre's first cousin so I know that if it ever came down to it her loyalty would be to me.

Keanna was the one who first told me about Dre and Alexus. Supposedly, they met at her graduation party. I was at the party too, but that never stopped my husband from being the dog that he was. I know they often wondered how I showed up to most of the places they went to and I had Keanna to thank for that too. I just had to promise never to let anyone know that she was my informant. Keanna had always been a good friend to me, but I didn't always return the favor. If she knew some of the things I had done behind her back, she probably would have never spoken to me again and Dre would definitely leave me.

According to Keanna, Dre had been dealing with Alexus for about two years. I use to hear things about her but I wasn't worried at first. Dre had cheated so many times that I knew the routine. Once I would find out he was cheating whoever the bitch was that he was with would be history. This was the only time that I felt like I had some real competition. She was a very pretty girl and she had body like a video vixen. I was intimidated by her but I would never admit that to anyone. I was far from perfect, but I was a damn good wife and mother to our four kids.

Dre and I had two girls and two boys ages eight, six, five and three. Dre always had doubts about our three year old being his. He claimed that he had barely been out of jail for a month when I got pregnant and I must have been sleeping with somebody else. I'll admit that I had needs and I did do me when he was locked up, but I was sure about the father of my kids. Dre was locked up so much I had to get sex from somebody. Hell at least I did it when he was locked up and not all in his face like he did me. He didn't try to hide his relationship with his mistress. My husband was actually in love with another woman and it was tearing me apart.

I felt like I was constantly being compared to a younger woman. And that was another problem I had. She was eight years younger than I was with no kids so of course her body was in near perfect shape compared to mine. She had also graduated high school and was now in college. That was something that I never did. Dre was constantly on my back to do something, but I didn't have any interest in anything. He had always taken care of me so I never needed to work. I hated school so going back was not happening. Keanna tried getting me to take Certified Nursing Assistant or CNA classes with her, but I wasn't about to be cleaning shit off of old people for $8.00 an hour.

My phone vibrated in my hand shaking me from my troubles. Keanna was calling me, probably with more drama. I answered trying not to sound as bad as I felt.

"Hello," I said cheerfully.

"Girl what's up with y'all over there? I just saw your husband outside the club talking to Eric and he looked pissed. Y'all must be into it again," Keanna said.

"Yep. When you told me you saw him and ol' girl getting out the car at Copeland's I went around there and waited for them to come out and followed them."

I told Keanna everything that took place starting at the gas station up until when Dre choked me and left. As usual, she always made me feel worse.

"Girl, you crazy. He's probably going right to Alexus. You know that's where he goes every time you make him mad."

I really didn't need to hear that but she was probably right. There was nothing I could do about it. Even though I knew where the condo was, I didn't know the exact one she lived in. I followed him there before but security wouldn't let me in without an exact location. I still couldn't believe he even bought the bitch a condo. And to make matters worse, it was in an expensive area on St. Charles Avenue in uptown New Orleans. I wasn't in the mood to talk about Dre anymore so I quickly changed the subject.

"So when are we going shopping for the barbecue?" I asked. Dre's dad was on his way to a halfway house in New Orleans in two weeks so Keanna and I were planning a barbecue at my house to welcome him home. I wanted everything to be perfect. I had met Dre's dad before, but just like his son, he was in and out of prison most of the time so we never really got a chance to bond.

"I guess we can start getting the decorations tomorrow. I know Deanna and Erica might want come too. They're so happy that their daddy is finally coming home," Keanna replied. Deanna and Erica were Dre's sisters and my girls. Most of the time when I went clubbing they were right there with me. They hated that bitch Alexus just as much as I did.

"So Dre cool with it being at y'all house? Didn't he say he wanted to do it at a park?" Keanna asked me.

"Girl, we're doing it right here. He probably just wants it at the park so that ho can come. He gon' get that bitch hurt one day!" I yelled. Keanna laughed.

"That's his heart right there. You know he's not letting you get too close to that girl. He acts like she's fine china or something." This was the only reason I hated talking to Keanna sometimes. I felt like she would sometimes rub Dre's infidelity in my face. She was always making comments about how much he loved Alexus or what he did for her. Things I really didn't want or need to hear. I was no longer in the mood to talk so I decided to wrap up our conversation.

"Well girl it's late and I'm tired as hell. I guess we'll talk later. Call me when you wake up so we can go to Party City to look at some decorations."

"Alright then. I'll let my cousins know just in case they want to tag along," she said before disconnecting the call. Keanna was my girl, but sometimes I found myself questioning whose side she was really on. It was like she took pleasure in my pain. She can side with the enemy if she wants to, but family or not she can get it too. As of now, Alexus was at the top of my list. She was playing a grown woman's game and I was determined to make sure she lost. I refuse to lose my husband to her or anybody else.

Chapter 4
KEANNA

I hate Cherika's trifling ass. She walks around talking like she is the perfect wife and mother. I have so much dirt on her; I could start my own desert. She is a grimy bitch and I have the proof. Cherika is so in love withDre until it was ridiculous. Dre has cheated on her so many times, it's hard to keep track. Most of the time, I hooked him up with females I knew.

I was the one who hooked him up with Alexus at my graduation party. I figured it would be just like any other time. He would wine and dine her, get some pussy and keep it moving once Cherika found out. He fooled me this time. Hell, he fooled everybody else too. He actually fell head over heels in love with the girl. It's almost like he's obsessed with her. He has to know where she is and who she's with every minute of the day. I only wanted to piss Cherika off, but this was even better. I am happy to do anything that causes her pain.

Cherika isn't used to competition. Whenever Dre cheats, he always makes his way back home. The side chick would be a distant memory until the next one came along. Cherika prides herself on being the wife. It's like she doesn't care if Dre cheats. She always says that once Dre gets his nut, he doesn't want them anymore. That was before Alexus came into the picture.

Alexus, her best friend Jada, and I graduated from the same high school. We used to hang out a lot and I really liked her in the beginning. That all changed after a while. Alexus is spoiled. She loves to shop and my cousin makes sure she stayed fly. Alexus is the youngest of six, so she always has to have her way. And most of the time she gets it. Especially from Dre's sprung ass.

I hate going places with her since men seems to be drawn to her like a magnet. I even caught my man Troy looking at her with lustful eyes. That was one line she better not ever cross. I have been with Troy since I was fifteen years old and now I'm twenty-two. He is my first love. He is my first everything. He is all I've known for the past seven years and I can't picture my life without him in it. In the beginning, things were really good. My man was making money with Dre while I worked at a nursing home from two to ten. We weren't hood rich, but we lived a comfortable life. Our bank account was straight so that was good enough for me.

I knew that Troy was most likely doing me like Dre was doing Cherika. I just couldn't prove it. He started coming in late at night, leaving early in the morning and the phone would ring non-stop. He always claimed it was business, but I knew better. My intuition told me it was another woman. I also noticed for some strange reason, he started feeling some kind of way about Dre.

He started saying things that made me think he was jealous of my cousin. Anytime Dre bought something new, he would complain about him being too flashy. If he and Alexus came over to our house, Troy would say how wrong Dre was for cheating on his wife. He just always had something negative to say. Whenever I checked him about it, we would always end up fighting.

I guess Dre felt it too because he eventually backed away from him. He no longer wanted to do business with Troy and we started hurting financially because of it. I knew that Troy was wrong, but I was upset with Dre. I was his cousin so he should have helped my man out on the strength of that alone. I was ready to crawl back to Dre and beg for his help when the unthinkable happened; Dre went back to jail.

Things seemed to get worse for us after that. Troy started selling weed with some white boys that he was hanging with. Even still, he never had any money. I was stuck paying all the bills and we were barely making it. He would stay out for days at a time. Money was missing from our savings and even my jewelry started disappearing. My family told me they thought he was using drugs. I just didn't want to believe it.

I toldErica about everything that was happening and she came up with a great idea. She helped me to install mini cameras throughout my house so that I could see everything for myself. The cameras recorded everything I missed while I was at work. The first week, I was too scared to view the tapes. I thought I would be better off not knowing. I knew that I wasn't going to leave Troy no matter what the tapes revealed. I lied wheneverErica asked me about it. I always told her that I didn't find anything unusual. The truth was that I never even looked.

That was until Troy disappeared on me for two days. No phone calls or nothing. I called every hospital and prison in the New Orleans area, but still came up empty. I decided then and there that I owed it to myself to know what he was up to.

My hands trembled as I inserted the disc into the computer. I pressed play and instantly regretted the decision I made. My house was turned into a drug-infested whorehouse when I went to work. I cried through two hours of heartbreaking surveillance of my boyfriend and none other than my cousin's wife, Cherika doing things that were only seen in a porno. They were like dogs in heat as they had sex in my bed, sofa, and kitchen counters. The bitch had the nerve to walk around my house naked like she paid rent there. The way he looked at her was the way I once looked at him, with love.

The worst part of it all was the amount of drugs they consumed together. So much white power went up their noses; it was a miracle that nobody overdosed. I had my suspicions about Troy using drugs, but I couldn't believe Cherika was using too. She never lost weight and her appearance never changed. They had pulled the wool over my eyes, but this tape made it all clear.

It all made sense to me now. The way Troy defended her when she and Dre got into arguments, the sudden change in his attitude towards my cousin all made sense now. He was fucking the man's wife. In my house, in my bed. All while she played the role of a faithful, loving wife, she was cheating too. I was too embarrassed to tell anyone about what I found. I held everything in, but I vowed to make Cherika's life a living hell. I couldn't believe that she could consider herself my friend after all of that. I even suspected her youngest son might be Troy's.

He didn't look anything like Dre or Cherika, but he bared a strong resemblance to my boyfriend's nephews. Troy's sister, Tara had two sons that looked exactly like Cherika's youngest son. Not only that, the tapes showed that they were intimate up until the day before Dre was released from jail. I never saw them use protection once, so there was a strong possibility that Troy was the father of Cherika's son Drew.

Dre had doubts from day one and I was determined to bring the truth to light. I wanted Cherika to feel the pain that she inflicted on me and much more. Losing Dre was her greatest fear. He was her weakness. I was about to make that fear a reality. I hated Troy just as much. His day was coming sooner than he thought. I was hoping that Dre would act as his punisher once everything was revealed.

I pulled up in my driveway after a night of clubbing and stared at the package in my hands. I stopped at a twenty-four hour Walgreens and purchased a home DNA kit. I don't know when or how I was going to do it, but I was going to get the job done. Getting a swab of Troy would be easy. He stayed high so much, he wouldn't feel a thing. Getting to baby Drew was going to be the challenge. He wasn't old enough to know what was going on, but if the other kids saw, they would rat me out. I was sure of that. I would have to sit down and figure everything out later. I dropped the package in my purse as I prepared to exit my car. It was time for me to put my plan into action. It was time for me to inflict pain on others as they had done to me.

I dreaded going inside because I never knew what to expect. Troy was sweet and loving one minute and beating my ass the next. I guess the drugs made him that way. When I walked in the house, I didn't see Troy in his usual place on the sofa. I prayed that he was already sleeping so I didn't have deal with him tonight. Living with him was becoming unbearable. I walked in our bedroom, turned on the light and the fireworks started. Troy jumped in my face screaming,

"Bitch, where you been? And why you out there with that short ass dress on?"

"I told you earlier I was going out with some of my co-workers. What's the problem?" I replied with attitude.

"Bitch, who you hollering at? You must want me to beat your ass in here!"

I refused to respond. I wasn't going to give him any reason to put his hands on me. I started taking off my jewelry, when Troy came up behind me and started kissing the back of my neck. I flinched at his touch thinking he was going to hit me. It was worse than I thought. He wanted sex.

Troy and I weren't intimate very often and I hated the times that we were. When he was high, it would last forever. Other than that, it was over in five minutes. He was always rough with me and I never enjoyed it. he didn't appear to be high Tonight so I was looking forward to a quickie. I guess he thought kissing my neck was foreplay, but that was worse than the sex. His saliva dripped down my back and made my skin crawl. He raised my dress up to my waist, pulled my underwear to the side, and forcefully entered me from behind. He never bothered to see if I was wet, which I wasn't.

"Shit," he grunted while power driving himself into me. I held on to the dresser waiting for him to be done with it.

"You like that baby?" Troy asked me. I knew from past experiences to tell him what he wanted to hear, so I did.

"Ooh yes daddy. I love it. Fuck this pussy!" I moaned. My fake screams of pleasure must have motivated him as he went deeper and harder. I tried to speed up the process as I threw my ass back at him just as fast. I guess my plan worked because two minutes later he pulled out and shot cum all over the back of my dress. I was disgusted. I wanted nothing more than a hot shower and my bed. I needed time to think of a master plan.

"Come take a shower with me," Troy said while entering the bathroom. This was not what I had planned. I undressed and went to join him in the shower where he brutalized my pussy for the second time that night. I replayed the tapes of him and Cherika in my head over and over again. It was crazy how he wanted to fuck me, but make love to another man's wife.

I climbed in bed once our sex session in the shower was over, but sleep was nowhere on my mind. Troy came out only to grab his "feel good" box from under the bed. That was the name I had for the cigar box he kept his drugs in. I knew he couldn't go a night without it. This would be the perfect time for me to get the sample I needed. Troy would sometimes sleep for twelve hours straight. I only needed thirty seconds to do the swab. I just had to make sure it was really lights out before I made a move.

I lay in bed with my eyes closed waiting for the right time to move. Troy had been out of the bathroom for over an hour. I knew he was in the living room because I heard the TV. I got up slowly and made my way down the hall to the living room. Troy was sprawled out on his back with his mouth hanging open.

I made a mad dash to my bedroom to get the DNA package from my purse. I opened the box with shaky hands and got the items that I needed. As I crept back into the living room, I was careful not to make a sound. Suddenly Troy coughed, causing me to drop to my knees. My heart was beating out of my chest. I stayed on the floor silently praying that he didn't wake up. After about ten minutes of quiet, I peeked up from my crouching position to see Troy in the same position as before. It was now or never. I had to move fast before I lost my nerve.

I crawled over to where he was and pulled out the cotton swab. I gently swabbed inside his mouth and cheek area while counting to thirty in my head. When I was done, I raced backed to my room and sealed the swab in the bag that was provided. I wrote in the required information and secured everything in my purse once again. I was relieved that I had at least got one part of it over with. I just needed to figure out a way to get the other swab. I was hooking up with Cherika later in the day. I was hoping to get her son alone for at least a minute.

I went to sleep with a smile on my face. I knew that it was only a matter of time before Cherika's world came crashing down.

Chapter 5
ALEXUS

I braced my hands on the headboard of our California king sized bed as I rotated my hips to the sensation Dre was giving me. I straddled his face and moaned in pleasure while he licked my love box expertly. Dre held my hips firmly in place to keep me from running away from his tongue-lashing. My eyes rolled back in my head as I released and fell over on my side, unable to sit upright any longer.

"I know you didn't tap out on me," Dre laughed as I scooted away from him.

Dre and I had been holed up in our condo for the last two days sexing each other like rabbits. I was drained. I needed to get out of the house and today was the day. I felt like I was suffocating. Jada and I made plans to hit up the mall, but I had yet to run it by Dre. He seemed to always have a problem whenever I went somewhere without him.

He had been so pre-occupied with his dad's homecoming and I hoped like hell he had something planned for today. There was no way he was coming with us. I had my own agenda so I wasn't going to offer. I had recently started talking to my ex-boyfriend again. I ran into him the night Cherika and I had the fight at the gas station, and we have been talking ever since.

When Jada picked me up from my sister's house, we went to the daiquiri shop and I saw Malik there. We talked for a while and he ended up coming back to Jada's house with us. Talking to Malik felt good. We didn't have a bad break up. He went to school in Virginia and we decided that a long distance relationship wouldn't work. He probably would have stayed the night at Jada's if Dre hadn't been blowing up my phone. I called him back and pretended to be asleep, but that didn't work. He still ended up coming to get me after two in the morning. Malik was meeting us at the mall and I needed to get a move on. First, I needed to let Dre know of my plans for the day.

"Jada and I are going to the mall for a little while."

"Yeah?" Dre asked. "What you need from the mall? You got shit in the closet with tags on it."

"I know that, but I still want to go to the mall," I replied. "I might see something else I like." He just looked at me and I know he was looking for something else to say. He was so predictable.

"You need some money."

"Nope," was my simple reply.

"What you mean no? Where you get money from?"

"I have money in my savings, Dre. You put money in there every month, remember?" I was feeling like I was talking to my father and not my man.

"I told you not to touch that money unless it's an emergency. If you need something, tell me." This was the shit I hated. I was the youngest of three brothers and two sisters and everybody treated me like a damn baby. Dre was the worst of them all. I didn't have an independent bone in my body because everybody did everything for me. I couldn't even cook a decent meal if I wanted to. He would take me out to dinner before he let that happen.

"Well I guess I need money then," I said with much attitude. I got up from the bed to get my clothes out for the day. I was still naked and I could feel Dre's eyes on me the whole time. I hurried to the shower before he tried to pull me back in the bed.

Once I showered and got dressed, I called Jada to let her know I was ready. Dre was on the phone with his dad, but he walked over and handed me a stack of money. His dad was due to come home the following weekend and he and Keanna were excited. Dre's dad and Keanna's dad were brothers. Keanna's dad died when she was six so her uncle, Eric Sr. or EJ, as they called him, took care of her. They were both going crazy buying him clothes, shoes and preparing for the barbecue they were giving him. Dre wanted to do it at the park so I could be there to meet his dad. Of course, I wouldn't be going since it was at his house. He asked me to, but I declined. He always used Keanna as a cover up whenever he invited me places because we were friends, but his house was off limits.

I got a text from Jada saying she was outside, so I grabbed my purse, kissed Dre, and walked out the door. As soon as I got in the car, I called Malik to let him know we were en route to the mall. I was excited to see him again, but I was nervous about Dre finding out. Even though he was married, he was adamant about me not being with anybody else. Dre never hit me and I didn't want it to ever come down to that.

Jada and I parked near the food court of Lakeside Mall. We waited for about ten minutes until Malik pulled up. Malik spoke to Jada and gave me a big hug. Malik knew about my relationship with Dre, but he didn't really care. He said that since Dre was married, I was fair game. The three of us walked into the mall discussing which stores to hit up first.

After about three hours and two trips to the car, we were finally done. We decided to get something to eat at the mall's food court. We all ordered Chinese and found a table to relax. Malik ate with one hand because he kept his other arm around me the entire time.

"Hey Lex," somebody said from behind me. I almost died when I turned around and saw Keanna standing there with a smirk on her face. What's worse is who she had with her.

"Yes Indeed." Cherika's hood rat ass laughed. I'm sure she was excited to see her husband's mistress with another man. I already knew I was busted. There was no doubt in my mind that she was going to rub this in Dre's face. It was all good though. I would never let that bitch see me sweat.

"Hey y'all," I happily spoke back. "What you doing in here Keanna?"

"I'm still shopping for Uncle EJ."

"Oh yeah, he'll be home next week huh?" I said that to get under Cherika's skin. She was standing there looking at me with a sour expression on her face. Malik still had his arm around me and I didn't try to move it.

"Girl yes and I can't wait." Keanna said while looking at Malik. "Don't I know you?" she asked him. "Malik right?"

"Yeah. You remember Malik. We used to talk in high school." I answered for him. Since I knew Cherika was going to tell it all, I at least wanted the bitch to get it right.

"Hey Jada," Keanna spoke to my bestie.

"Hey," Jada said dryly. Jada didn't care for Keanna too much. She thought she was dirty for hooking me up with Dre and still being friends with his wife.

"You ready to go friend?" Jada asked. Her timing was perfect. I was more than ready to bounce. "Well girl, I'm about to go. Let me know if you need help with your uncle's party." I know she didn't need help, but I loved to put the wheel in Cherika's back.

"She's good. I'm helping with my father-in-law's party," Cherika responded putting emphasis on her statement. That shit was funny, so I laughed as I walked away. I know that bitch was watching so I grabbed Malik's hand and switched my fat ass extra hard. All I had to do now was sit back and wait for "Hurricane Dre" to make landfall.

Chapter 6
D'ANDRE

I didn't know what was up with Alexus, but I would find out eventually. She was on some sneaky type shit lately. I know something was up with her I just didn't know what it was. When she was in the shower earlier, I noticed she had a lock code on her phone. Something she has never done in the two years we were together. I went back to sleep for a while after she left, wondering what she was up to.

I decided to go see my mom and sisters when I woke up. I got there and noticed that my kids were already there. That wasn't anything new. Cherika always dropped them off over here while she ran the streets. They ran over to me, almost knocking me down when they saw me. They were excited and I felt bad because I never really spent any time with them. My sisters D'Anna and Erica were sitting on the sofa when I walked into the living room. They went off As soon as they saw me, talking about Alexus.

"How you gon' let that lil bitch disrespect your wife like that D-Mack!"

"You wrong for that shit!" "And you letting the hoe drive your car now too?" Since they were both talking the same time, I addressed them at the same time.

"First of all, her name is Alexus, not bitch or hoe. And don't worry about who drive my car or what I buy. I don't ask y'all for shit. I take care of me!" They had me all the way fucked up.

"Wow!" my sister Erica said. "You gon' lose your wife behind some bullshit."

"So. Like I just said, don't worry about me!" I yelled, pissed off. My mama came downstairs wondering what everybody was hollering about. My sister Deanna told her and she started too.

"Dee you know you wrong for doing Cherika like that. That girl loves you to death and you treat her like a dog." "That lil girl is not worth losing your family. You don't know what she out here doing." For some reason, everybody wanted to be in my business. I was mad even though I know my wife put them in it. Mutherfuckers don't know shit unless you tell them.

"Man, it doesn't matter. Y'all are worrying about the wrong thing. I'm a grown ass man. I'm not forcing Cherika to stay with me!" I came over here to see my family, but it was time for me to go.

"Alright. Don't say I didn't warn you. You can't play with people's hearts like that, Dee. That girl gon' end up hurting you."

I love my mama, but damn. She was forever preaching to a nigga. I let her have that one. I couldn't win an argument with her anyway. She didn't approve of me being with Alexus, but she was never ugly with her like my sisters. She always called her that little girl, unlike my sisters, who referred to her as a bitch or a hoe. They never said anything disrespectful to her face, but they went off when she wasn't around. I hadn't talked to Alexus since she left to go to the mall with Jada. I wanted to call her, but I sent her a text saying "I Love U" instead. I just prayed she wasn't playing games with me while I'm sitting here defending her to my family.

I decided to take my kids and chill with them for a while. That was something I had to do more of. Cherika and I were so preoccupied with our lives and we never made time for them. They told me they wanted ice cream so that was where we went. We got our ice cream and went to the park to eat it.

I needed this time with my kids. My daughters, Denim and Dream, were entertaining me by singing and dancing. D'Andre Jr. was playing on the slide, but Drew stayed under me the whole time we were at the park. Even thought I had my doubts about him, I would never treat him any different from my other kids. I was the only father he knew and I still didn't have proof that I wasn't.

My pops had been gone for five years so he had never met my sons. Cherika was pregnant with Lil Dre when he got locked up and of course, Drew wasn't born yet. I was so excited that my pops was coming home.

This would be the first time in a while that we would be home at the same time. We both stayed locked up so much. I couldn't wait for him to meet my baby girl. I knew he was going to love her. We made sure he had everything he needed when he came home.

It was getting dark so after about two hours, I rounded up my crew and headed home. I sent Cherika a text letting her know that they would be home with me. I just hoped she didn't get too happy and rush home. I wasn't in the mood for her nagging ass. After I helped them take a bath, they sat in the TV room and watched movies while I ordered a pizza. Looking after four kids was not a joke. I said I didn't want anymore, but I wasn't so sure after meeting Lex. I could definitely see my baby girl carrying my seed one day. She wasn't feeling having kids yet so she took her birth control faithfully. My plan was to hang around here until they went to sleep. After that, I was going to get my baby and head to our spot. I know I would have to hear Cherika's mouth because I haven't slept home in two days.

Alexus and I had been inside for the past few days sexing each other like crazy. My wife and I haven't slept together in a few months. She would give me head most of the time to keep me from leaving the house, but that shit never worked. It was crazy how I felt like I was cheating on Alexus every time I was with my wife. My baby girl definitely had me open. There was no denying that.

I was lying on the sofa surrounded by my kids when I heard Cherika come in. She had a few shopping bags in her hands, which was no surprise.

"Hey Baby," she said. I don't know what was up, but she was happy and smiling.

"Hey," I spoke back dryly. I guess she went to put her bags away because she came back empty handed. She sat next to me and started talking.

"Me and Keanna were in the mall and guess who we ran into?" She said it like a question, but she answered it herself.

"Alexus and her boo." My heart dropped. She was happy as hell to share that info with me.

"Who?" I asked. I just know she didn't say Alexus.

"Yes, your boo Alexus was in the mall with her boo. Kissing and all hugged up and shit," she rubbed it in.

"Yeah?" was all I said. I would never let her know that she was getting to me. For all I know she could've been lying. She must have read my mind because she kept talking.

"You think I'm lying? Call Keanna, she'll tell you. I think she know him too." Now she really had my attention even if I don't show it. I needed to know what she was talking about. I was ready to go after that. I had some people I needed to holler at. I wanted to talk to Keanna and I especially wanted to talk to Alexus sneaky ass. I hopped up and told her that I would be right back after I made a quick run. That was a lie. I had no intentions on coming back tonight.

I calledKeanna as I drove on the Mississippi River Bridge in route to Jada's house. She pretty much told the same story that Cherika had told. The only difference was she gave me a name. According to her, Alexus was in the mall with her ex, Malik. Last time I heard that nigga was in Virginia going to school. Now I was really pissed. I was wondering how long this shit had been going on. Alexus lied to me. Now I knew how my wife felt when I did her wrong. I swear it felt like I couldn't breathe. This feeling was new to me and I didn't like it at all. I told her not to play games with me, but I guess she wasn't listening.

I drove in front of Jada's house to see if anything looked unfamiliar to me. That's when I spotted a black Maxima with Virginia license plates. I knew it had to be that nigga car. I kept driving and made the block. I parked my car a few houses down so I wouldn't be noticed. I called Alexus and put her on the speakerphone. I wanted to hear what she had to say, even though I know it was going to be a lie.

"Hello," she answered on the second ring.

"Where you at?" I asked even though I already knew.

"I'm at Jada's house."

"Well what time you coming home? You want me to pick you up?"

"No, Jada is bringing me home," she replied quickly. I had no intentions on picking her up. I only said that to scare her. My plan was for her to rush ole boy out of the house so I could follow him. I wanted to see what he had to say too. I decided to ask her some questions while I had her on the phone. That way I could compare their stories to see if she was lying.

"Let me ask you something and please don't lie to me," I said in a calm tone.

"OK," she said sounding nervous.

"What nigga were you in the mall with today?"

"I was in the mall with Jada, but we ran into Malik when we were in there." I know she was lying, but I let her keep digging her own grave.

"I knew your messy ass wife was going to try to start some shit!"

"So you wasn't hugging and kissing on that nigga?" I asked.

"What! No! I wasn't hugging and kissing nobody. I know you don't believe her of all people." I expected her to say that. Any other time I would have fell for it, but my cousin co-signed Cherika's story. "So that's the story you sticking to? I'm giving you a chance to tell me the truth. If I find out something different, we're gon' have a problem." I gave her a chance to get it right.

"It's not a story. That's the truth." That was the story she was sticking to and I had to accept that. "Alright. I'll see you later. Don't be over there too long," I said as I hung up.

I sat in my car and patiently waited. I knew Alexus too well. She was scared. She didn't want me to pop up on her so she was about to rush ole boy out the door. And just like I thought; the porch light came on and somebody opened the screened door. Alexus stepped on the porch followed by a tall, light-skinned dude. They said a few words to each other and he stooped down and gave her a long hug. That nigga was too familiar. He was rubbing on her ass and everything. I was heated. It took everything in me not to get out the car and fuck both of them up.

Just as she turned to go back inside, he pulled her back, bent down, and kissed her. Not a peck on the lip kiss either. This nigga had his tongue in her mouth. And the fucked part was she was kissing the nigga right back. I saw all I needed to see. There was no way in hell she could make me believe that she just ran into that nigga today. Alexus finally pulled away and went back inside the house. Ole boy got in his car and pulled off with me right behind him. I didn't know or care where he was going.

We ended up on the Westbank Expressway, going towards Harvey and Marrero. I followed him for another fifteen minutes and I had a feeling that this fool was going to Pee-Wee's. That was my brother and my little cousin's stomping grounds. Just as I thought, his dumb ass pulled into Pee-Wee's parking lot. I sat in my car for a while, giving him time to get settled in. I called my brother while I waited. He and some of my cousins were already inside.

I finally got out of my car, checking to make sure I was strapped in case something popped off. I found my family taking up two tables at the back of the bar. I made my way over to them, while scanning the club for Malik. I spotted him and two other dudes sitting at the table drinking Heinekens. I sat down next to my brother and started telling him and my cousins why I was there. My little cousins were rowdy. They wanted to go over there and get it popping. I didn't have a problem with that; I just wanted to talk to him first.

I waited for a few minutes before I got up and made my way over to his table. I pulled up a chair and took a seat right next to my target.

"What's up? Malik right?" I asked. He looked at me strange, but he nodded his head letting me know that I was right.

"I'm Dre. I'm sure you heard about me before, right?"

"Yeah, I heard of you," he said trying to play cool in front of his boys. I could smell the fear all over his scary ass.

"Look, let me holler at you in private for a minute." I guess he didn't want to go nowhere with me because he asked his boys to leave. That was cool with me.

"I'm not trying to beat around the bush with you; I'm trying to see what's going on with you and my girl." I wasn't into playing games. I needed to know what the deal was.

"Nothing going on with us," was his nervous reply. I wasn't buying it so I kept pressing him.

"So you just happened to run into her in the mall today?"

"Naw, I ran into her and Jada a few days ago at the daiquiri shop." "We just been kicking it and talking on the phone ever since. I met them at the mall earlier."

This nigga was singing like a bird. Alexus was doing the damn thing for real.

"So she didn't tell you she had somebody?" I had to know if she lied about that too.

"Yeah, but she said you got a wife. I just figured she was free to do her since you were married." Wrong answer. I almost gave the nigga a pass. He just signed up to get his ass whooped.

"I hear you my dude, but I need you to hear me too. I know you and Alexus had y'all lil thing a while back and all, but that's over. I'm coming to you myself so you don't have to hear it from nobody else. Lose Alexus's number and forget you even know her. I promise you this is not what you want. You look smart so you know what I'm saying." He didn't respond, but I hope he got the point.

"Sorry for breaking up your lil party, homie. The next round is on me," I said as I walked away. Alexus was going to be the death of me. I was on my way to our spot because she had a lot of explaining to do. I walked back over to my little cousins just as Malik's friends made their way back to the table.

"He's all yours," I told them as I left the bar. They jumped up like the building was on fire and dashed over to Malik and his friends. The last thing I saw before leaving was a chair going across Malik's head, courtesy of my cousin Quan.

Chapter 7
ALEXUS

I finally made it back to the condo and I was exhausted. I was expecting to see Dre there since he rushed me from Jada's house. I was so scared that he was going to show up while Malik was there. I hurried Malik along to make sure that didn't happen. I gathered my things and prepared to take a shower. I was ready to crawl in my bed. As I showered, I thought about the conversation Dre and I had earlier. He made it seem like he knew more than he said he did. It was hard for me to lie to him. It seemed like he always knew when I wasn't telling the truth. I hope like hell that I did a better job of it this time around. Cherika was so stupid. She should have been happy that I had somebody else besides her husband. I guess she figured he would leave me alone if he knew about Malik. I got out of the shower and oiled my body before putting on some boy shorts and a sleeveless tee. Dre hated when I slept in pajamas.

Once I was done, I started putting away everything I got from the mall earlier. Dre walked in just as I put up the last of my purchases. He walked in the room, but didn't speak. That was unusual for him. He was always happy to see me. I was just about to say something, when out of the blue, Dre slapped the shit out of me. The impact was so hard; it sent me flying to the floor. I was shocked. I tried to scoot away, but he bent down and he slapped me two more times.

My face was stinging as tears clouded my vision. I couldn't believe it. Dre never hit me before. He threatened me a lot, saying he would, but he never did. Was this over what his wife had told him? If so, I was done with his ass. I didn't have to wonder for long. Dre leaned over me and forced me to look at him while he spoke.

"I asked you a million fucking times to tell me the truth!"

"You've been talking to this nigga for a while." How in the hell did he find that out? Jada was the only other person that knew and she would never tell him anything.

"You fucked that nigga?" He was in my face screaming.

"NO!" I yelled. Malik and I kissed a lot, but we never had sex. Dre already knew he was my first. He pulled my hair, forcing me to stand up and look at him.

"I know you were kissing that nigga. Now lie and say you weren't!" This was too much. He knew everything. He finally let my hair go and threw me on the bed.

"Give me that phone," Dre yelled.

I jumped up from the bed and got my iPhone from my purse, handing it over to Dre.

"Take this damn lock code off."

I did as I was told. If he read any of the text message between me and Malik, shit was about to get real. I got back in bed and pulled the covers up to my neck. I was scared that he was going to hit me again. Dre took my phone with him when he left out of our room. After crying for what felt like hours, sleep finally came to me.

When I woke up, it was after ten in the morning and Dre wasn't in bed with me. I didn't know if he was even in the house. I was starving, but I was scared to leave out of the room. I got up and went to the master bathroom to do my morning hygiene. When I got back in the room, Dre was sitting on the bed, fully dressed.

"Get dressed," he said calmly.

"Since I can't trust you to be by yourself, you rolling me with today." I wanted to tell him that I didn't need babysitter, but I wasn't stupid. I got dressed and waited until it was time to go. I still hadn't eaten anything, but I would starve before I said something. At this moment, I regretted my decision to take the summer off from school. Anything was better than this. I wanted out of this relationship. I just didn't think Dre would leave without a fight.

Once we left the house, Dre stopped at the Waffle House and got me some breakfast. He must have known I was starving. We made a million stops after that. He bought food and a million other items for his dad's party that was coming up. When he pulled up to his mothers' house, I almost died. This was the last place I wanted to be. Nobody in Dre's family liked me except his brother Eric. I hated being around them. I was hoping we didn't have to get out of the car. Dre called his two nephews to the car to come help with the bags. When they saw me, they started smiling. These little bastards made me sick. They were always looking at my ass when they saw me. After they got everything from the car, opened the passenger door for me to get out. I couldn't keep quiet so I said what was on my mind.

"What we over here for? I hate coming to your mama's house," I said. He grabbed my hand as we walked up to the front door.

"I need to take care of something. It won't take long." When we walked through the front door, all eyes were on me. If Dre hadn't been holding my hand already, I definitely would have grabbed his. "Good Evening," I spoke to his sisters who were on the sofa along with his mother. None of them bitches opened their mouths.

"Damn, y'all can't speak?" Dre said with an attitude.

"Hey," they said like they were being forced. Dre sat on the other sofa and pulled me on his lap. The whole room fell silent. I was so uncomfortable and more than ready to go. He did shit like this on purpose. He knew how his family felt about me, but he still bought me around them. I listened as they talked and made plans for their father's party.

The party was supposed to be at Dre's house, but it appears to have been moved to his mom's house judging from the conversation they were having. I couldn't wait until we left so I could ask Dre why it was moved. It seemed like they would have more food and alcohol than anything. After they were done talking, Dre and I prepared to leave.

"Dre, let me talk to you for a minute," his mother said. Dre had my hand so I tried to let go so he could talk to his mom. He gripped mine harder and pulled me right along with him. I could tell that she wanted him to come alone because she hesitated to speak. She looked from me to him several times, but didn't say anything. I know she wanted me to leave, but he had a death grip on my hand.

"You called me back in here to stare at me?" Dre called her out. He made it clear that I was staying right there.

"You know your wife and kids are gonna be here Saturday right?" she asked Dre.

"Yeah, I know. What's that mean?" I knew what it meant. She was telling him not to bring me, but she didn't have to worry about that. I didn't want to be anywhere near her or her daughters.

"I'm just saying," she replied before walking off.

"We out!" Dre yelled.

As soon as we got in the car, I started asking questions.

"Why did you move the party over here?" I asked.

"So you can come and meet my pops." He said that like it was nothing.

"Dre, I am not coming to your mama's house. I can see if it was at the park or something. That's a public place." He must be crazy to think I would go there for anything.

"First of all, that's my shit. They just live there." Dre was quick to remind everybody that the house his family lived in was his. I know that was the only reason they never said nothing when he bought me there. The house was still in his name so they knew not to piss him off too much.

"Dre, I can meet your daddy some other time. It's not that serious. I'm not trying to be fighting with nobody."

"You gon' meet him Saturday and nobody ain't gon' fuck with you! Believe that," he said. I guess this conversation was over. His mind was made up. Dre came with a lot of unnecessary drama and I needed to get away from him before it was too late. After he put his hands on me the night before, I was more than ready to call it quits.

Saturday was finally here and I was at my mother-in-law's house getting everything ready for my father-in-laws homecoming celebration. Dre was picking him up from the bus station at four and it was almost noon. I knew he was going to our house to shower and change clothes so that would buy us some more time. I was still pissed with him. His sisters told me that he came over here with his bitch the day after I told him about her and another nigga. And I noticed that he was in his truck, but his car wasn't at home. I had a feeling she was driving his Benz, but I wasn't sure. If so, we were going to have some serious problems.

For some reason Dre didn't want his dad's barbecue at our house. I had a feeling he was on some bullshit. I know he better not disrespect me and bring his bitch around here or it was going to be on and popping. I wanted to make a good impression on Dre's dad. We met before, but we never got a chance to spend time around one another. I was hoping that maybe he could talk some sense into his son about our marriage. He didn't listen to the rest of his family, but he and his dad were very close.

I was going crazy. Dre still stayed out some nights and we rarely spent time together. I was sexually frustrated because we no longer had a sex life. Not unless you count me sucking his dick from time to time. He never protested when I did that. I guess Alexus' young ass didn't do it right, if she did it at all.

Keanna and I were putting table clothes on the tables when Dre and Eric walked in the backyard. I wanted to know where his car was so I asked him.

"Where's your car at Dre?"

"Why?" He said with an attitude.

"I want to know that's why!"

"Don't worry about nothing you didn't buy." His ass was always throwing money in my face. I got money when he was locked up and I can get money now. I chose not to do a lot of shit because I really love my husband. It was sad that he didn't show me the same love and respect.

"I know your bitch better not be driving it," I said while pointing in his face.

"You better keep your damn hand out my face. And so what if she does drive my car. That's my shit." Eric was laughing, but I didn't find a damn thing funny. This nigga was really going to make me hurt him. There's only so much a person could take. Sometimes I felt like he was better off in jail. I didn't have all of these problems when he was locked up.

Keanna and I went back inside to finish helping with the food. She was starting to piss me off a lot too. She was always talking to Alexus when I was around. She made sure that I knew who it was because she kept saying her name. She was messy as hell and I was just realizing it. As soon as she hung up, she started with her foolishness.

"Girl, don't say nothing, but you know Dre trying to get her to come over here to meet Uncle EJ." I kind of figured that anyway. I know Dre better than anybody. That's why he didn't want us to do it at our house. I would have killed that bitch if she would have step foot on my property. I was still going to whip her ass if she came over here too.

"Don't worry about it girl. She probably won't even come. She said she don't want to come anyway. That's him with all that." Keanna said. Dre was pathetic. It wasn't even that serious behind a bitch.

Finally everything was done. A lot of people were there and more were expected to come. Dre had already picked up his dad. They were at our house getting dressed. Dre was like a woman when it came to that. He had to make sure he was perfect. I loved that about him. They were due here any minute. I sat outside with my sisters-in-law talking to all of the guests when my daughter ran through the yard telling us that her dad was here. I was a little nervous about meeting Dre's dad again. I didn't know what he told him about me or our marriage. They walked in the yard and I was in shock. Dre was a younger version of his daddy. Dre introduced him to our kids and they were so happy to have a Grandpa. My dad died when I was eleven so this would be the only one they had left. I didn't get up from my seat. I was waiting to see if Dre was going to introduce me to his father. After what seemed like forever, he finally made his way over to me.

"Pops you remember Cherika right?" Dre asked his dad. I was kind of disappointed at his introduction. I wanted to be introduced as his wife, not Cherika.

"Yeah I remember my daughter-in-law," his dad responded with a smile.

I was smiling so hard after he said that. We hugged and he sat down next to me in a lawn chair. We talked about the kids and my marriage. He didn't say what I thought he would say. He felt like I let Dre do the things he did to me. That was far from the truth. I didn't want my husband to cheat, but I couldn't stop him. Everybody's solution was for me to leave him. That was never going to happen and I wish they would stop suggesting it.

After a few hours, the party was in full swing. Everybody was full and the alcohol was being passed around. Keanna, my sisters-in-law, and I were sitting at the table playing cards while the kids ran around the yard. Some of the guest left, but a few were still there. I noticed Dre and his dad disappeared a while ago. I assumed they were inside the house, but I had a feeling that something was up.

When our game was over, I went inside the house to search for my husband. Dre wasn't downstairs so I went upstairs to check for him. After coming up empty, I went back downstairs and saw Keanna peeking out of the window. I stood beside her to see what she was looking at. I almost died. My dog ass husband and his dad were outside talking to Alexus.

And the worst part was Dre's Benz had suddenly appeared. I knew it. He let that hoe drive his car. I hated to act a fool in front on Dre's dad, but he left me no choice. I ran outside with Keanna and Dre's sisters hot on my heels.

"I know you don't have this bitch out here knowing I'm right inside the house." I yelled walking up to Dre.

"Y'all really got me fucked up!" I walked over to where they were standing. Dre had the nerve to be standing in front of that bitch like he was protecting her or something. Dre's sister Erica was going off too while his dad tried to hold us back. Keanna just stood there and watched.

"Move out of the way Dre. You don't have to stand in front of me," Alexus said. That was it; I snapped and reached around Dre to grab her. Erica tried to get to her too, but they were holding her back. Alexus reached around Dre and grabbed my hair. Before anybody knew what happened, we went into a full-blown mix. She was getting the best of me, but I still held my own. Erica was trying to break free from her dad to jump in, but he wouldn't let her go.

"Erica I wish you would!" Dre yelled at his sister. I was furious. Was he really taking up for this bitch?

After a few minutes of brawling, Dre and his dad were finally able to pull us apart. My kids were on the porch crying so Keanna and D'Anna took them inside. Dre pulled Alexus to the car trying to make her get in. If I could kill somebody and get away it, she would be my first victim. I hated her for ruining my marriage. Dre's dad carried me into the house and sat me down on the sofa.

"You alright?" he asked.

"No, I'm not alright. Your son is gonna make me kill him!" I said to my father-in-law as I got up and went upstairs. As far as I was concerned, he was in on it too. I just wanted to get my kids and go home. I was so tired of Dre embarrassing me. I had been in so many fights over the years due to his infidelity. He just didn't care about anybody else's feeling, but his own. It was only a matter of time before he got tired of Alexus too. I ran up the stairs searching for my kids. It was time for us to go. I found Lil Dre, Denim, and Dream in the room with Deanna.

"Where's Drew?" I yelled in frustration.

"Keanna took him to use the bathroom," Deanna replied. I started gathering our things when Keanna came in with Drew. I picked him up as my other kids followed me down the stairs and out the door.

Chapter 9
KEANNA

I finally did it! I got both of the swabs I needed to have the test done. While Cherika and Alexus were fighting at my uncle EJ's party, I was able to get a DNA swab on Drew. He was too young to know what was going on. He thought we were playing a game so it was a piece of cake. I opened a P.O. Box at the post office so the mail wouldn't come to my house. I didn't want anyone to know what I had done. Troy would kill me if he found out. The results were due back any day now. I went to the post office every day; sometimes twice a day.

I talked on the phone with Cherika while in route to the post office to check the box yet again. She was happy because Dre had been home for the past three days. That was only because Alexus and her family went to ATL to visit her brother who lived there. As soon as Alexus came back, Dre would be gone again. Cherika was so stupid. Dre disrespected her in the worst way. I think he wanted her to leave him, but that wasn't happening. She had lots of fights over my cousin, but she had met her match with Alexus. She thought Lex couldn't fight, but she soon found out that she was dead wrong.

I pulled up to the post office and went to open my box. I rummaged through some junk mail until I spotted what I had been looking for. Cherika was happy now, but all of that was about to change. Troy was indeed the father of Drew by 99.6 percent. Tears fell from my eyes as I read over the results. I hated them for doing this to me, but I would have the last laugh. I told Cherika I would call her back as I pulled up to the public library.

Once inside the library I borrowed some white out. I used it to cover up my customer information at the top of the DNA form. I then made three copies and put them in envelopes. I didn't know what I was going to do with two of the copies, but one of them was definitely for Dre. I just had to find a way to get it to him without him knowing it was me. I wondered how he was going to handle the situation. He was already looking for a reason to leave her and I was going to help him out. I wanted her to hurt just as bad as she hurt me. Losing Dre to Alexus was going to kill her. She loved him more than she loved herself.

Funny thing was, he loved Alexus like Cherika loved him, but I don't think Lex felt the same way. I still didn't know how to handle the situation with Troy. I love him and hate him at the same time. I was scared of being alone so I know I wasn't going to leave him. I talked about Cherika, but I was no better. Troy put me through so much with the drugs and beatings, yet I stayed with him.

After riding around for what seemed like forever, I decided to call Cherika back to see if Dre was still at home. I had to find a way to get a copy of this test to him. Maybe I could leave it on the windshield of his car. That was kind if risky though. Somebody could come outside and catch me. "Hello," Cherika answered on the first ring.

"Hey girly, what you doing?" I asked her.

"Nothing at all. I'm bored as hell in here."

"Where's Dre?" I asked, hoping he was gone.

"He went to the barber shop. At least that's what he said," she responded.

That was perfect. Dre only let one person cut his hair and that was our cousin, Derrick. They would be in the shop for hours joking and playing video games. Cherika said he had only been gone for about an hour. I knew he would probably be there all day. It was now or never. I hung up with Cherika and headed over to the barbershop. I spotted Dre's car backed into a spot at the store across from the shop. I drove around the block a few times just to see if anyone was outside.

Once I saw that the coast was clear, I made my move. I grabbed the envelope from my purse and secured it under the windshield wiper on the driver's side of the car. It would be the first thing to catch Dre's eye when he got in. I hated to hurt my cousin like that, but he needed to know that his wife was a no good, grimy bitch. I could breathe easy now that the hardest parts were over.

All I had to do now was sit back and wait for the shit to hit the fan.

Chapter 10

D'ANDRE

I had been at home for the past few days spending time with my kids. My baby girl was in Atlanta visiting her brother and I missed the hell out of her. I was so happy that she was coming home tomorrow. Cherika was driving me crazy so I decided to go to one of my barbershops and chill.

My cousin, Derrick, ran the place for me since he was a licensed barber. I only used the place to wash my dirty money, but the profits were damn good. After being there for a few hours, I said my goodbyes and prepared to go home.

When I got to my car, I noticed a white envelope stuck under my wipers. I looked around to see if anybody was watching me. I didn't see anything out of the ordinary so I grabbed the mail and hopped in my car. At first I thought it might be pictures, but the envelope was too light. I was curious about what it was so when I stopped at a red light, I tore the envelope open and pulled a piece of paper out.

"What the fuck!" I said aloud to myself.

The car behind me honked its horn. I didn't even realize the light had turned green. This had to be some kind of joke. According to the papers in my hand, Troy was Drew's biological father. This was no joke. There was no mistaking the truth that stared me in the face. This paperwork was definitely official. How else would Troy and Drew's full names be on it?

It appeared that whoever wanted me to see this didn't want their identity revealed. I noticed that the customer info section at the top was blank. I didn't have a clue who it could be. I really didn't care at this moment. I've always had doubts about Drew being mine, but Troy never crossed my mind. It all made sense to me now. That's why that nigga went left on me. He was fucking Cherika. I wondered how long it had been going on. I really didn't know how to feel at this point. Troy was like a brother to me at one time. That pissed me off more than anything.

A part of me felt like both of them did me a huge favor. There was no doubt in my mind that Cherika and I were history. I was looking for a way out and she gave it to me. I wasn't even going to wait until morning to leave. I was going to get my shit and bounce tonight. The house was dark and quiet when I walked in. I knew my kids were sleeping and I was happy that they wouldn't see me leaving. I know Cherika wasn't going to let me go without a fight, but I was prepared.

I went into our bedroom and headed straight for the walk-in closet. I knew I wouldn't be able to take everything tonight, but I wanted to get the most important things first. Knowing her ghetto ass, the rest would probably go up in flames before morning. Cherika was lying in the bed watching TV. When she noticed that I was packing my clothes, she jumped up and started screaming at me.

"Dre what the hell are you doing?"

"Man, Cherika I'm out. And don't start all that screaming and shit before you wake up the kids." I knew that wasn't going to happen.

"What you mean you out? How you gon' leave your kids for another woman Dre? What am I supposed to tell them?" She started crying, but I wasn't falling for that shit.

"First of all, I'm not leaving them, I'm leaving you. And this don't have anything to do with Alexus. This is all on you."

"What's all on me? I have done nothing, but try to keep my family together. You're the one who bought a third person into our marriage."

"You ain't done nothing, huh?" I asked.

"No I haven't," she cried.

"Ok. So answer this for me. Who were you fucking when I was locked up?" She had a surprised look on her face that she quickly erased.

"I wasn't fucking anybody! I don't know who you been taking to, but somebody is lying on me."

I continued packing. My mind was made up. No matter what she said, I was leaving.

"So you saying you never had sex with Troy?" She kept her face straight this time when she lied to me.

"What! I never had sex with Troy. Who told you that?" I was done talking. She would never tell me the truth anyway. I went in my pocket, pulled out the DNA paper, and held it up for her.

"So since you never slept with him, these DNA results saying he's Drew's father by 99.6 percent must be a lie too." This time she couldn't hide the look of shock on her face. She looked at the results and quickly came up with another explanation.

"That shit is fake! Somebody probably photo shopped that or something. When did anyone get the time to test Drew? That's bullshit!" she screamed.

"So why him, Cherika? They could have picked anybody and said they were Drew's father. Why would anyone just randomly pick Troy?" She wasn't making any sense to me.

"Baby I don't know, but that's a lie. Drew is your baby." She retorted.

"Prove it. Let's take another test," I suggested. I knew she would never go for that.

"Why you doing this, Dre?" She cried. "You just trying to find any reason you can think of to be with Alexus."

"Like I said before, this don't have anything to do with her. You giving me all the reason I need to leave your lying ass. Just tell the truth Cherika. That's all I'm asking you to do."

She sat on the floor crying, but she didn't respond. She was proving her guilt and didn't even know it.

I grabbed the two duffel bags that I packed and prepared to take them to my car. Cherika jumped up and blocked the door so I couldn't leave.

"Move out the way Cherika. Don't even play yourself." I told her. She was about to start acting a fool, I could tell.

"Dre, please don't do this!" she cried falling to her knees.

I stepped over her and walked down the stairs. I put the two bags in my trunk and went back to get some more. When I got back upstairs, I noticed Cherika wasn't in the room. I used this opportunity to take as much as I could before she came back. I grabbed another duffel bag and filled it with shoes. I decided to come back later for everything else. I heard voices coming from down the hall so I assumed Cherika was on the phone calling one of her sisters. I would be long gone before any of them got here. ˙

After checking the closet one last time, I grabbed my bag and headed for the front door. I got downstairs and had to do a double take. Cherika and all four of the kids were sitting on the sofa downstairs. I could tell that she had woken them up because they still looked tired.

"Daddy, don't leave us," my oldest daughter cried. I looked at Cherika in disgust. She was using my kids to get me to stay.

"I'm not leaving you baby, I just need to get away tonight." I told my daughter. She was only eight, but that didn't matter to Cherika. She would use a dog to get her way. My kids should have been in their beds sleeping instead of getting caught up in our drama.

"Don't lie to her. Tell her you're trying to move out on us," Cherika said as tears fell from her eyes.

If my kids weren't down here, I would have slapped the shit out of her. I put my bag down and sat on the sofa next to my daughter. I hated to see her cry. If making her happy meant leaving a little later, then that's what I would have to do. I turned the TV on and watched cartoons with them for a while. I could feel Cherika staring at me, but I refused to look her way.

After a while, the kids were sleeping peacefully once again. I looked over at Cherika and said what was on my mind.

"You're a poor excuse for a mother. Why would you do that to them? That's fucked up, Cherika."

She sat there wiping away her tears, but she didn't respond. I got up and started bringing the kids upstairs to their rooms. I hope she didn't think I changed my mind. I was still leaving.

Once the kids were in their rooms, I prepared to dash the scene again. I grabbed my bag and started for the door.

"Dre wait!" Cherika yelled. I stopped to hear what she had to say. "I'll tell you whatever you want to know, just please don't leave me!" she cried.

"Cherika, it's late. You wait until two in the morning to decide you want to talk," I said as I left.

I heard her break down as I walked out the door. This time she didn't try to stop me and I didn't look back.

I went back to the condo and unpacked all of my clothes. Alexus would be home later today and I couldn't wait. I wanted to call her, but it was too late so I sent her a text instead. I wanted to make sure she came straight here before going anywhere else. We had a lot to talk about. I needed to tell her about everything that happened while she was gone.

I never did apologize to her for putting my hands on her, but the thought of her being with somebody else enraged me. It felt like she started pulling away from me after that. I couldn't let that happen. I would do whatever needed to be done to make her happy. I needed her more than she knew. I didn't want to be with nobody else. Not even my own wife.

Chapter 11
ALEXUS

We were on our way back to New Orleans from visiting my brother, Allen in Atlanta. It felt so good to get away from all the madness in my life. I honestly didn't miss Dre one bit. I did miss my bestie though. I talked to her every day while I was away. She was the only one that knew about Dre hitting me. If my brothers knew, they would go crazy. Jada and I finally figured out how he found out some of the things he knew. Malik would never answer when I called, but he did answer for Jada. He told her everything that happened the night he left her house. Apparently, Dre saw him at the bar and they had words. Malik was the one who shed light on how long we had been back in contact with each other. Thanks to Dre, I lost a good friend and Malik had to have his jaw wired. It wasn't Dre who attacked him and his friends, but I know he was responsible for the attack.

Dre sent me at text early this morning telling me to come straight to our spot. He said we had a lot to talk about. I really wanted to go to my mom or my sister's house, but I knew he would have a fit. I didn't need him showing up at any of their houses looking for me. I guess I could spend today with him since Jada invited me to her family's seafood boil the day after.

Alex was pissed that I wanted him to drop me off at Dre's house, as he referred to the condo. He hated Dre more than anybody else. Alex was the oldest out of the six of us. He was extremely overprotective of me. He was very outspoken so I never knew what to expect when it came to him and that mouth of his.

When we pulled up, I hurried out of the car to grab my bag. I didn't want Alex to get out. I went to the driver's side and gave him a kiss, telling him that I would call him later. As soon as I got up the stairs, Dre opened the door and pulled me into a tight hug. He picked me up and grabbed my bag as he walked inside with me in his arms. We went into the master bedroom and I noticed something was different. Dre had a lot of his clothes and shoes lying around the room. He always kept clothes here, but this was way more than usual. He laid me down on the bed and started taking my shoes off. I wasn't in the mood for sex right now. I wanted to know what the hell was going on. When he started removing my shorts, I stopped him.

"Dre, what's going on?" I asked.

"Why are your clothes all over the room like this?" He ignored me and continued trying to take my clothes off.

"Dre, stop," I said again more forcefully. I could tell he was mad, but I didn't care. I needed some answers. Dre sat on the bed next to me and told me everything that took place over the last few days. He even showed me the paternity test that somebody left on his car. I couldn't believe Cherika and Troy slept together. I was having an even harder time believing that Troy was Drew's father. Some things just weren't adding up.

"Dre, I think you should do another test. This is weird. Who could have tested Drew without y'all knowing?" I was trying to make sense out of a crazy situation.

"I don't know." Dre said. "I wouldn't just go by what that paper says," I told him.

"Maybe you can make an appointment somewhere else to have it done again."

He didn't respond, but I know he was thinking about it. This was all too much for me to handle. I didn't need these kinds of problems. I was ready to leave Dre and all his drama behind.

The next day, I decided to clean the house and wash all of our clothes. Jada was picking me up in an hour to go her cousins' seafood boil. Jada's twin cousins, Katina and Katrina, were the same age as us. We hung out sometimes, but this would be my first time going to their house. They were sweet girls who always made me feel welcomed. Dre was walking around with an attitude ever since I told him that I was leaving. He was starting to get on my nerves. I didn't tell him to leave his wife and I damn sure didn't tell him that I would be living here with him permanently. I refused to sit inside under him all day.

"What time you coming back?" Dre asked as I was getting dressed.

"I don't know," I responded with a hint of disgust in my voice. I was not Cherika. D'Andre Mack was not the center of my universe.

Jada sent me a text letting me know that she was outside. I grabbed my purse and prepared to exit stage left, when Dre grabbed my arm.

"Damn, I can't get a kiss?" he asked. He leaned down and forcefully stuck his tongue in my mouth, almost gagging me. "You better be good," he said as he released me. I walked out the door without replying. I still loved Dre, but I wanted a break. I was feeling suffocated.

I got in the car with Jada smiling from ear to ear.

"What the hell are you so happy about?" Jada asked.

"I'm happy to be getting the hell out of that house. I just got back yesterday, but I'm ready to go again," I responded.

"Girl, that man is not letting you go nowhere. You stuck for life," Jada laughed. I didn't find it funny because it was true. No matter how many times I tried to leave Dre, he always made his way back into my life. That was nobody's fault, but my own.

When Jada and I pulled up to her aunt's house, there were cars everywhere. I didn't expect so many people to be here. It kind of made me nervous, but I didn't let it show. I was happy that I decided to look extra cute today. I wore my yellow Chanel romper with my yellow and grey Chanel ankle strap wedges. We walked into the yard and I felt like I was on display. All of Jada's male cousins eyed me like a piece of meat as we passed. Jada stopped to introduce me to a few of them. I made sure to stay close to her as we searched around for the twins.

"Girl, you got my cousins foaming at the mouth with all of that ass you got." Jada laughed.

"I didn't know this many people would be here," I responded. We went into the house and found the twins in the kitchen with Jada's aunt, Tyra. Tyra was the twins' mother, but she looked damn good for her age. Trina and Tina were her youngest at twenty-one, but she had another son who was twenty-six that I had never met. Jada and the twins always talked about him. That was the only reason I knew he existed.

"Hey pretty girl," Tyra smiled as she spoke to me. She always called me *pretty girl* whenever she saw me. This was my first time at her house, but she was always at other family gatherings that I went to with Jada. She was always nice to me no matter where we were.

"Hey Ms. Tyra," I said.

"Girl, I told you to stop calling me Ms. I am not that damn old. Just call me Tyra," she said while snaking her neck.

"Hey y'all," the twins spoke.

"Hey," we replied in unison. We sat around in the kitchen laughing and talking with them for a while.

"Ma!" someone yelled from the front of the house.

"I'm in the kitchen," Tyra yelled back. I heard footsteps coming our way and then he appeared. I had to force my mouth closed as I stared at the specimen before me. He was tall with light skin and pretty gray eyes. I tried not to stare, but damn it was hard. When our eyes locked, I quickly looked away, but he didn't.

"Helloooo," Tyra said, getting his attention.

"Oh, um where you want me to put the liquor at?" he asked.

"You can bring it in here," Tyra responded. "And this is Jada's friend Alexus. Lex this is my oldest son Tyree," Tyra introduced us. We spoke to each other as he exited the kitchen.

"Well damn," Tyra laughed as she looked at me. I blushed, but she was right. Her son was fine as hell.

"Where is the bathroom?" I asked to no one in particular.

"It's the first door down the hall to the left," Tyra answered. When I got up, Tyree and another man were entering through the front door.

"Damn," one of them said as I passed by. I splashed some cold water on my face before I left the bathroom. I really had to get it together. The last thing I needed was to meet somebody else right now. I still had a mess on my hands with Dre. I would never be able to forgive myself if I dragged another innocent person into my mess. I felt bad enough about what happened to Malik.

Jada, the twins and I, sat in the yard eating seafood and drinking wine coolers. I didn't know what Tyra did for a living, but she had a beautiful home with a huge yard and pool. There were a lot of people here and they still had room for more. Tyree and some of his cousins were playing dominoes at a nearby table. I noticed that he kept sneaking peeks at me, but I pretended not to pay attention. Jada noticed too and made the twins aware of it.

"Look at how Ty keep looking at Lex on the slick," Jada laughed.

"Girl, you gon' be our new sister-in-law!" Trina chimed in laughing.

"No ma'am," I replied. "I got enough on my plate."

"Yeah, she got her own real live stalker," Jada said. We all laughed at her statement, but it was the truth. Dre had either called or texted me every half hour since I left home. He wanted to know what I was doing or how long I was going to be out. After a while, I stopped answering for his insecure ass.

As the time passed on, most of the guests started to leave, but a few family members were still hanging around. I was having fun so I wasn't in a big rush to go. It felt good being with someone other than Dre. It was dark outside so everyone was scattered throughout the house doing different things. We were in the kitchen playing cards when Tyree came in and sat down at the table with us.

"What?" Tina asked him.

"What you mean what?" he replied.

"Why you in here?" She countered.

"I can come in here if I want to," he laughed.

"You think you slick," Jada said. "I know why you in here." The twins started laughing.

"It's about time you made your move," Tyra said walking in the kitchen.

"You've been asking about her all day." Tyree put his head down, embarrassed.

"Can I talk to you for a minute?" he asked me.

"Outside," he countered. I got up and followed him outside as Jada and the twins clapped and laughed loudly.

"What's up?" I nervously asked once we were in the yard.

"I just wanted to get to know you, that's all. Tell me something about you." I told him a few things about me, leaving out the part about Dre. I knew he would ask me that soon enough.

"So you got a man Alexus?" I knew that question would come up. I don't know why, but I felt comfortable enough to tell him about my situation with Dre. I just hoped he didn't judge me or look at me differently.

"What about you? You got somebody?" I asked.

"Not really. I mean I do have a few female friends that I chill with, but I'm not in a relationship at the moment," he replied. Tyree and I stayed in the yard and talked for over an hour before Jada came out and said she was ready to go. It was after eleven and she had things to do the next day. I wasn't ready to go, but she was my ride.

"Can I get your number?" Tyree asked before we left.

"I'll get one of my sisters to ask for you or something. I don't want your man to get mad," he smiled.

I took his phone from him and programmed my number in. I then called my phone and stored his number in under his sister Trina's name. He laughed at my gesture and told me to make sure I use it. Tyree hugged Jada and I after he walked us to the car. We said our goodbyes and were on our way. I was not looking forward to going home. I know Dre was going to be pissed. He called me non-stop for the last two hours, but I didn't answer any of his calls. I was enjoying my night and I didn't need him to ruin it.

When Jada and I pulled up to the condo, Dre was out front waiting for me. I was sacred as shit, but I wouldn't dare show it. Jada asked if she should wait, but I told her I was good. As soon as she pulled off, he started with his bullshit.

"You really got me fucked up Alexus!" Dre screamed.

"I know you saw me calling your sneaky ass!" He grabbed my arm and pulled me inside. It pissed me off when he called me sneaky. After all, he was the one who had a wife.

"I was playing cards Dre. I couldn't answer the phone every time you called," I replied.

"Your ass is lying! You were probably with a nigga!" I tried to break free from his grip, but it was too tight.

"Dre, let me go," I cried. He let me go and threw me on the bed. When I tried to get up, he pulled me back down and held me in place with his forearm. I panicked when he started trying to remove my clothes with his free hand.

"You fucked him?" he yelled.

"What are you talking about Dre?" I was scared of what he was going to do, so I started swinging wildly, trying to push him off of me. The blows I delivered had no effect on him at all. He reached between my legs, unsnapped my romper, and removed my underwear. *Is he trying to rape me*, I thought to myself. I was terrified.

"You probably still have that nigga's scent on you," he said as he sniffed my underwear.

I never felt so hurt and degraded before in my life. Tears filled my eyes as I jumped up from the bed preparing to pack my belongings. I was leaving and I had no plans to return.

"Where the fuck are you going?" Dre asked, following me to the closet.

"I'm leaving," I cried.

"I'm done with you. I swear I regret the day I met you!" I could barely see as the tears clouded my vision. Dre pulled me out of the closet and hugged me tightly from behind.

"You not going nowhere. You know I'm not letting you leave," he whispered.

"This is not working Dre. I need some space. You are too insecure." He still didn't let me go. I could barely move because he was hugging me so tight.

"I'm sorry baby. I know I'm insecure sometime. But I promise to work on it. Just give me a chance to get it together," he pleaded.

"I think we need a break from each other Dre. This is all too much for me. I don't think it's meant for us to be together." I was trying to get him to see things my way. He turned me around to face him and I couldn't believe what I was seeing. He was actually crying. I don't know why, but a part of me felt sorry for him. Dre never cried about anything.

"Don't do this to me, Lex," he cried. "I love you to death baby. I promise I'll do anything to make this right with us baby."

As much as I wanted to push him away, I couldn't do it. I really did love him even though he drove me crazy at times. When Dre noticed that I was no longer putting up a fight, he led me over to the bed and laid me down. Before I could protest, he kneeled down, pushed my legs back to the headboard, and buried his face deep inside my treasure. I grabbed his head and pulled him in deeper as I rotated my hips. And just like every other time, Dre had me under his spell and all was forgiven.

Chapter 12
D'ANDRE

I was so happy that things were back to normal with me and my baby girl. I couldn't lose her over any foolishness. That would kill me. Alexus was my heart. Hell, she was the only female that has ever reduced me to tears. That shit still shocked me sometimes. I was never one to cry over a female. I would just move on to the next one. Our last argument was the biggest one we've ever had. I spent over a month making it up to her and we were better than ever. I know I was a little insecure at times, but I was trying to work on it. I don't know what kind of hold she had on me, but I couldn't imagine her with anybody else.

I took Alexus's advice and had Drew retested. Just like the first one said, I was not the father. I confronted Cherika with the second set of results, but she still denied sleeping with someone else. She was still trying to get me to come back home, but that would never happen. The only time I went there was to get my kids. I still treated Drew like he was my own. I was the only father he knew. Besides, it wasn't his fault that his mama was a hoe. I lost count of the number of times I asked her for a divorce. She acts crazy every time the conversation comes up.

That nigga Troy was locked up, but I was going to see him as soon as he got out. I wasn't salty about him sleeping with Cherika at all. I could get pass that. I couldn't get pass the way he just cut me off after I treated him like a brother. For some reason, I felt like Keanna had her hand in all of this too. It had to be somebody close to me in order for them to make this happen. She had access to Troy and Drew, so she was suspect number one in my book. I tried calling her a few times, but she never answered. In my eyes, she was guilty until she could prove me wrong. Lex didn't think she had anything to do with it, but I wasn't convinced. She played the role of friend to Cherika and was stabbing her in the back at the same time. She knew I would leave Cherika if that info ever got out. The thing that pissed me off was how she did it. She could have come to me like a woman and told me what she knew. It was all good. I knew I would run into her sooner or later.

"What you want to get into today?" I asked Lex as we lounged on the sofa. We hadn't really spent any time together for the past few days. I had the kids for a few days and she was hanging with Jada a lot lately. I wanted her to stay home, but I couldn't do her like that. I was trying to get better with my trust issues. I know it wouldn't be fair for me to keep her inside with me and my kids all day.

"I want a tattoo," she said, shocking the hell out of me. Alexus was scared to death of needles. I had so many tattoos, I lost count, but she didn't have any.

"What kind of tattoo you want?" I asked.

"I want a butterfly," she said smiling. My baby was so pretty. I couldn't tell her no even if I wanted to.

"Alright, we can do that, but you better not be in there crying. You know you're scared of needles," I told her.

"Just hold my hand and I'll be alright," she said.

"I got you, baby," I replied. I scrolled through my phone and called my boy who did all of my tattoos to make us an appointment.

We pulled up to the shop a few minutes later than our appointment time, but it didn't seem to be too crowded. I stopped at the daiquiri shop and got Alexus something to drink for her nerves. I could tell she was scared, but she was the one that asked for it. We walked into the shop and I wanted to turn my ass right back around. Of all the days, Charde had to be in here today. She was sitting at the counter with some of her ratchet ass friends. She looked Lex up and down then started whispering to her friends. I grabbed Lex's hand and hollered at my boy.

"What's up Joe?" I spoke.

"Ain't nothing. What you getting done Dre?" he asked me.

"I don't know yet, but my baby wants a butterfly on her back," I told him pointing to Alexus. I could feel those bitches staring at us, but I ignored it.

"Y'all can look in the books and see if it's something she likes in there," Joe told us. "Damn Dre, you can't speak?" Charde asked louder than she needed to.

"Nope," I simply replied. This junkyard dog looking bitch was about to piss me off. We sat down and looked through the books that Joe gave us until Lex saw a big colorful butterfly surrounded by smaller ones that she fell in love with. When she got up to show it to Joe, Charde got up too and purposely bumped into her. I jumped up just in time as Alexus pushed Charde back into the counter. "Damn!" Joe laughed as he put a covering over his client's new ink.

"Dre, you better control your bitch," Charde yelled.

"The only bitch I see in here is you," I said as I mean mugged her and her flunkies.

"Yeah, I'm a bitch until you want some head," she replied with a smirk on her man looking face.

"No this bitch didn't put me on blast like that," I said to myself. It was no secret in the hood about Charde's mean head game. Niggas from everywhere got at her to get some of it too. Everybody knew that was my weakness so I let her swallow some of my babies from time to time.

"Yeah, you speechless now, huh?" she laughed. Her friend who Joe had just finished working on laughed loudly as they prepared to leave.

"Fuck you, Charde," was all I could say as they left. She won this round. I could tell that Lex was mad even though she maintained her composure. It wasn't even that serious to me. It wasn't like I hit it. Oral sex wasn't cheating in my book.

When Joe was ready to start on Lex, I sat in the chair next to her. I reached for her hand, but she pulled away. I knew right then that I was back in the doghouse. We've been doing good for over a month and now this shit had to happen. She didn't flinch at all when Joe was inking her up so I know she had to be heated. I sat there flipping through the books and decided to get me another one while I was there.

Joe finished with Lex. Her tat was bad as hell. She was looking at it in the three-way mirror while he went to get more supplies to cover it.

"You like it," I asked her.

"Fuck you Dre," she said angrily. "I knew you were a dog, but your wife's sister though?"

"That shit happened a long time ago," I lied. If she knew it happened since we've been together, she would leave my ass for sure. That was a chance that I was not willing to take.

"But you were still married to her sister Dre," she said while shaking her head.

"I was young and stupid Lex. I messed up. What else you want me to say?"

"I guess I need to prepare myself for whatever with you," she replied.

"Don't do that Alexus. I never gave you any reason not to trust me. I show you more respect that I show Cherika or anybody else." I can't lie and say that I never messed around with nobody else since I been with her, but she always came first. I made sure of that.

Joe came back in and was ready to get started on me. I guess Alexus didn't want to watch so she went to the front of the shop to sit down. I had to straighten this out and fast. I couldn't stand when she was mad with me. Joe and I made small talk while he drilled ink into my neck for my latest piece of art. I was happy that Alexus didn't stay to watch. I wanted to show it to her and see the look on her face. Joe was adding some color to it and we would be on our way.

Alexus and I stopped to get something to eat before going home. I didn't want to sit in a restaurant with a bandage on my neck so we got our food to go. She was quiet for most of the ride. I had to force her to talk and I was getting aggravated.

"Talk to me. I hate when you're quiet like this," I said breaking the silence in the car.

"I'm good," was all she said.

"You need to stop acting like a child," I said getting mad. Alexus was so used to getting her way. I couldn't get mad since I created the monster that sat before me.

"So I'm acting like a child because I don't agree with your whorish ways?" she asked sarcastically. "Man, like I said before, all of that happened before I even met you. You act like you looking for a reason to be mad. I can't take back anything that happened in the past." I reached over and grabbed her hand. I expected her to pull away, but I was happy that she didn't. That was a start, at least. When we got inside, we sat down to eat and watch TV. I was just happy that my baby was talking to me.

"So what kind of tattoo you get?" Alexus asked me when we finished eating.

"Why?" I countered back while smiling at her.

"Let me see it," she replied. I got up to sit in a chair in our dining room. I pulled her down on my lap so that we were facing each other.

"Take it off," I told her, referring to the covering over my tattoo.

"Don't rip it off. Do it slow." I held her around her waist as she gently removed the tape and gauze from my neck.

"Dre!" she gasped.

"You like it?" I asked her.

"Yes, I love it," she smiled while placing kisses all over my face.

I knew she would, that was my reason for getting it. Joe put Alexus's name on my neck in capital old English letters. He colored the inside of the letters red. It came out a little bigger than I thought it would be, but it was nice. I knew getting this tattoo was going to cause a lot of problems for me, but it was too late now. Alexus was a permanent part of my life just like the ink that was on my neck. I wouldn't have it any other way.

Chapter 13
KEANNA

Dre had been blowing up my phone for the past few days. I didn't know what he wanted with me and I didn't care. I know he left Cherika's conniving ass a few months ago and I was ecstatic. She called me a few times to cry on my shoulder. I had to put my phone on mute so she wouldn't hear me laughing. She has yet to tell me why he left her as if I didn't already know. She wants to make everybody believe that he left her for Alexus. That was partly the truth, but that wasn't his main reason for leaving. It killed her that he had their kids around Alexus.

According to her, the kids loved Alexus and always came home talking about her. If she was looking for sympathy, she was dialing the wrong number. This was only the beginning for her. I had enough on my plate right now with Troy being locked up. His bail was $20,000 and I had no idea how I was going to get the money. I was working like crazy, but I would never be able to save enough to get him out, plus keep up with our bills.

His family basically washed their hands with him, so calling them was not an option. If he was still on Dre's team, he would have helped with no problem. Troy did a lot of people dirty, so his list of supporters was short. They arrested him for possession and some other charges that I wasn't familiar with. Even though I was still mad about him and Cherika, I didn't want to see him in jail. I know I was stupid for even caring, but I couldn't help it.

"Good Morning," a male voice said from behind me. I knew that voice from anywhere. He was the owner of the building that the nursing home I worked for was in. He was also someone that I had my eye on for months. I didn't know if he had a wife or a girlfriend and I didn't care. I would gladly be the side chick.

"Good Morning," I replied sexily. This man made me nervous just looking at him.

"What are you doing up this early?" I asked.

"Me and my pops had to go over some paperwork with your boss. Looks like y'all might be in here for another five years," he said holding up the new lease that my boss signed. He and his dad owned several professional buildings as well as some homes and apartments. He told me a while back that he had a MBA in business management and a real estate license. I was impressed since he was so young. I would swear he was a dope boy just by looking at him. As the old saying goes, looks are deceiving.

"That's what's up," I told him.

"Y'all open y'all club yet?" I asked him.

"No, we're not opening a club. We're leasing one of our buildings out to a club owner. The club is his, but the building is ours," he replied. He was so cute. I could picture myself leaving Troy's broke ass for him. At least I probably wouldn't have to work. I know he had money from the way he dressed and the cars he drove.

"Is the club open yet? Maybe we can go check it out one day," I flirted.

"It's not open yet, but it should be in a few months. He's doing a grand opening. I'll let you know when," he said as he left out.

I couldn't stop smiling after that. If everything went right, Troy would be a distant memory. I deserved somebody who was going to appreciate me and not take advantage of my kind heart. I thought Troy was that someone. He turned out to be a drug-addicted dog. Maybe he needed to stay in jail. At least he would be able to detox and get some of that dope out of his system. My ringing phone snapped me out of my daydream. I looked down and saw that it was Cherika calling me. "Hello," I signed into the phone. I was not in the mood to be a part of her "I miss Dre" pity party.

"Hey girl," she spoke sounding like a wounded puppy.

"What's wrong with you?" I asked as if I didn't know.

"Going crazy, as usual. What you doing later?" she asked.

"Working," I simply replied.

"Oh. I was going by your auntie's house. Her and your grandma wants to talk to me and Dre about all this foolishness," she said.

"What foolishness? Y'all separated. What's to talk about?" I asked, getting disgusted. She was doing too much to get Dre to come back to her.

"I don't know. Hopefully they can talk some sense into his stupid ass," she said sounding hopeful. "Dre is not listening to nothing they have to say. His mind seems to be made up," I replied.

"You don't know that. He might listen to your grandma," she replied with an attitude.

"Girl let him be and find you somebody else. He's not the only man in the world," I snapped. I was already tired of having this conversation with her.

"I know that, but he's the only man I married. I don't want another man. I want my husband," she said putting emphasis on the word husband.

"Well girl I have to go. I hope everything work out for you. Good Luck," I said before hanging up. She was going to need a lot of luck to get Dre back home. I hope she had a rabbit's foot and a four-leaf clover somewhere. She was definitely going to need it.

Chapter 14

CHERIKA

I hate to call Keanna sometimes. She make me think she's in on the shit sometimes. In the beginning, it was she who told me any and every thing that happened with Dre and Alexus. At first, it didn't bother me because I was so used to Dre cheating. It was Keanna who made me realize that their relationship was more than his normal flings. So much was happening so fast and I didn't know who to trust anymore.

I still couldn't figure out who gave Dre a copy of a DNA test that was done on Troy and Drew. For some reason, I suspected Keanna of doing that too. Over the last few months, her attitude towards me changed. I wondered if she somehow found out about me and Troy. She had lots of opportunities to test her man and my son since she was around them both so much. That was the only scenario that made sense to me. I was stressed to the max dealing with all of the problems I was having.

I was on my way to drop my kids off at my mother's house. I had about two hours before I had to be at my mother-in-law's house so I wanted to talk to my mom for a minute. My mother and I didn't talk very often. I loved her to death, but she was always on me about one thing or the other. My mother, Brenda was a very spiritual woman. Whenever she talked to anyone, she would always take it back to the Bible. She believed in God's word and everything that it said. My sisters and I rarely missed a Sunday going to church when we were younger.

As we got older, we went our own way and did our own thing. My mama always told us that we had so many problems because we strayed away from the church. If I thought going to church would bring my husband back home, I would be there right now. Dre meant that much to me. It had been over four months since he left and the only time I saw him was when he came to pick up the kids. He answered his phone when I called, but if it wasn't about our kids, he would hang up on me. He still treated Drew like he was his very own even after two paternity tests proved that he wasn't. That only made me love him more.

I knew there was a possibility that Drew could have been Troy's, but I was praying that he was Dre's. Troy and I had been sleeping together while Dre was locked up. It started out with him helping me make extra money by selling weed. After a few weeks of hanging out with each other, one night, it just happened. It was never supposed to go as far as it did. It was understood that I would never leave Dre and I didn't want to hurt Keanna either.

Troy was the one who introduced me to drugs. We would snort coke and have sex at his house when Keanna was at work. I thought that was a secret that I would take to my grave with me, but my past came back to haunt me. As many times as I had forgiven Dre in the past, he couldn't forgive me this one time. He moved on with Alexus like I never existed.

To make matters worse, he was flaunting her in the streets like she had his last name. I was so tired of people telling me they saw them together. My sisters and all of my friends would call me all times of the day and night if they saw them out somewhere. I couldn't sleep most nights and my appetite was nonexistent. My weight dropped by at least thirty poundssince the day he walked out on me. I know that I was partly to blame for Dre leaving, but he was at fault just as much.

"Ma!" I yelled as we walked into my mother's house.

"I'm in the den," she yelled back. My kids took off running towards the den to greet their grandmother.

"Go upstairs and put y'all stuff in the bedroom. I got some ice cream cups in the freezer," my mama told my kids. I sat down on the sofa next to her and she started in on me.

"Why are you losing so much weight, Cherika? That can't be healthy," my mother said in a concerned voice.

"I'm stressing ma. I got a lot going on with me right now," I replied.

"Baby you need to pray. You can't turn anything around without HIS help," she said pointing to the sky. I knew this was coming. That's why I didn't come over here as much as she wanted me to.

"I know that, Ma," I said in a defeated tone.

"You can't put nothing or nobody before God Cherika. I always tell you that. I know you love your husband, but you can't make him love you back. You can't love him more than you love yourself."

I knew she was right, but I wasn't trying to hear that.

"He loves me, we're just having problems right now," I said.

"Cherika, Dre has been gone for a few months and it doesn't seem like he's coming back. He asked you for a divorce more than once and from what I'm hearing, he's running around town with that lil girl you always fighting with." My mother always managed to make me feel lower than I did before.

She continued "And what's this I'm hearing about him taking a DNA test on Drew?" I knew this would come up eventually. My sisters couldn't keep their mouths closed for nothing.

"Drew is not his, OK? Can we please not talk about this anymore?" I pleaded. I was ready to run back to my car and go anywhere, but here.

"So who is Drew's father Cherika?" My mother just would not give up.

"That's not important ma. Dre is the only father he knows and that's the only father he'll ever know."

"So is that the excuse he gave for leaving you and my grandbabies? Or did he just want to be with that other girl?" My mother was relentless, but that was the million-dollar question-a question that I didn't have an answer to.

"He didn't leave me to be with her," I said, trying to convince myself as well as my mother. It hurt too much to even think about him and Alexus being together.

"Well if that's who he wants to be with, let her have him. Give him his divorce. You can't hold on to someone who keeps letting go," she said.

"I'm not giving him a divorce. We'll get past this just like we got past everything else. I refuse to lose my husband behind this foolishness. " I yelled. I didn't mean to raise my voice, but I was tired of people telling me to leave my husband. Nobody knew what I was going through.

"You already lost him," my mother said, bringing tears to my eyes. I couldn't stay here a minute longer. I grabbed my purse and walked to the front door.

"I'm only trying to help Cherika. You're losing yourself behind a man and I hate to see what this is doing to you." I left after my mother's last statement. I hated how she could see right through me. She was the only person, other than Dre, who could bring out my emotional side. I was always cool on the outside, but I was a wreck on the inside. I'm all alone with nobody to talk to.

I sat outside my mother-in-law's house trying to regain my composure. I had been crying since I left my mother's house. The puffiness in my eyes was evidence of that, so I waited until I looked like my usual happy self before getting out of my car. I was praying for everything to work out like we planned it to. Dre's grandmother was the one who put this all together. She wanted to talk some sense into Dre without Alexus being around. He seemed to bring her everywhere he went.

His grandmother, Ms. Shirley, specifically asked him to come alone. She wanted Dre's dad to come, but he refused. I guess he already chose whose side he was on. Obviously, it wasn't mine. I really hadn't seen too much of him since his party a few months ago. He wouldn't say much to me when I did see him so I guess he was another player for team Alexus.

"Hey everybody," I spoke as I came through the front door.

Dre's mother, grandmother and his sisters were all sitting in the living room and two of his aunts and a few of his cousins were in the dining room. I was so happy that they were all here. I know that Dre's family had mad love for me. I was the one who held him down and had his back, no matter what. When he was locked up, they couldn't really do much for him. I made sure he was alright, no matter the sacrifice. That had to count for something.

"He should be on his way over here right now," Dre's mom, Leslie announced.

"I don't know what's wrong with my son. He acts like he losing his mind," she said sounding frustrated.

"We about to get his mind right," his grandmother said. I hoped she was right. I was at the end of my rope trying to get my marriage back on track.

We all sat around laughing and talking when Dre finally arrived with Eric in tow. They came through the front door and paused when they saw all of us in the living room.

"What's up?" Dre said to his grandmother.

"You said you wanted to talk to me. I didn't know the whole family was gon' be here."

"Well I asked everybody to come over here. We all want to talk to you," she replied.

"What is this supposed to be an intervention or something?" he asked while he and Eric laughed. "You can call it what you want, but this is no laughing matter," Ms. Shirley replied sternly. Dre and Eric stopped laughing and sat down on the sofa.

"What's going on with you, boy? You running around with that lil girl like you don't have a wife and kids at home." Ms. Shirley got right to the point.

"This girl has been here for you when nobody else was. Even when you cheated and went to jail every other week, she never left your side."

Dre looked at me with pity in his eyes. Maybe her words were hitting their mark. I desperately needed him to understand how serious this was to me.

"You have a good wife Dre. Both of y'all have made mistakes, but it's not too late to fix them," his mother chimed in.

I know she was referring to Drew not being his son. I already told Dre's family everything. I figured if I wanted them to help me, I had to put it all on the table. They didn't like it, but they assured me that they had my back. In their eyes, Dre had done far worse.

"I understand everything that y'all saying, but this goes beyond what y'all see," Dre finally spoke up. He looked at me and continued,

"I love you, but not the way a husband is supposed to love a wife. This marriage has been over for a while and we both know it. I can't even stay faithful for longer than a week. I was wrong for staying as long as I did knowing how I felt." I was crushed, but I still wasn't giving up.

"We were fine until you started messing with that bitch. Everything went downhill from there. You just used the situation with Drew as an excuse to leave and be with her," I yelled.

"Keanna told me about you and her a long time ago." I didn't care that I was giving up my source of info. She was on some other shit lately anyway.

"Keanna?" Dre asked while laughing. "Who you think hooked me up with her? I didn't even know Alexus before I went to her party," he replied.

I was pissed beyond belief. The main one, who claimed to be on my side, was the source of all my pain.

"So Keanna's messy ass hooked you up with her, but turns around and tells Cherika everything about y'all?" Dre's aunt asked.

"Exactly," I replied.

"How do you think I knew everywhere you went?"

"That's why she hasn't been coming around lately," Dre's sister Erica said.

"How did y'all expect the girl to react? You not only slept with her man, but you had a baby by the nigga too," Dre said looking at me. I really didn't care about Keanna at this point. She would get hers soon enough. We were here to discuss me and Dre's marriage so that's what I wanted to do.

"Look Dre, I don't care about all of that. We need to come to an understanding about us. Maybe we can go to counseling or something," I suggested.

"First thing you need to do is let that lil girl go about her business," Ms. Shirley said. "Alexus!" Dre yelled.

"What?" his mom replied.

"Her name is Alexus. Not bitch, not lil girl, it's Alexus or Lex." He looked like he was ready to go off on somebody.

"Wow. Really Dre? We're having a discussion about us and you worried about what people are calling her?" I asked my husband.

"I think both of you need to sit down and talk to somebody. My pastor does marriage counseling all the time. As long as you both agree to go, I can set it up for you," Dre's aunt said. That was perfect. I was ready to go whenever he wanted to meet with us.

"I definitely want to go," I quickly replied.

"What about you Dre?" she asked while looking at my husband.

"I don't want to go counseling," he replied as my heart stopped beating.

He looked at me as he spoke. "You know we talked about this already. Like I told you before, I appreciate you for everything you did for me. I'll make sure you and my kids don't want for nothing, but I'm not happy being married. Just sign the papers and we can both move on."

I couldn't hold my tears at bay any longer. My world was ending right before my eyes. I felt pains in my chest as I struggled to catch my breath. My mother-in-law rushed to my side and held me as I cried like never before.

"Dre, you're wrong for this shit. That young bitch is gonna do you the same way. Just wait and see," his mother spat angrily.

He lowered his head, but didn't respond. That's when I saw it. He had a tattoo with her name in huge red colored letters on his neck. It felt like I was having an outer body experience as I jumped up from the sofa and attacked Dre like the scorned woman I was. I punched, kicked, and scratched every part of his body that I came in contact with. It took Eric a while before he was able to pull me off of his brother.

"You got that bitch's name tattooed on your neck! Nigga, fuck you!" I screamed and cried as Eric led me away from him.

Dre got up and fixed his clothes like it was no big deal. I knew right then what I had to do. He would need me before I needed him. I would make sure of that.

"Let's go, Eric," Dre said as he walked to the door.

"You're wrong for that one, Dre. How you get her name tattooed on you like that? You forgot you're married?" Erica asked.

"Erica, mind your fucking business. Don't worry about what I do. I'm a grown ass man and I'm tired of telling y'all that," Dre yelled.

"Eric, I'm gone," he said as he walked out of the door.

Eric let me go and followed behind him. I dropped down to the floor, crumpled in a fetal position. The pain I was feeling was like nothing that I've experienced before. Dre not being a part of my life was never in my plans. For the past eight and a half years, he was all I knew.

He was the first man to take care of me financially and emotionally. I couldn't figure out where we went wrong. I did everything I thought I was supposed to do. I gave him his first child and the son that he always wanted. Sex was never an issue since I gave it to him whenever and wherever he wanted it. He only cheated because he was a dog. I tried not to give him any reason to roam, but he did anyway.

It only got worse when he started seeing Alexus. Before then, he would never stay out all night. He went out of his way to make sure I never caught him with another chick. When he got with her, he just didn't care anymore. My mother's words were ringing in my ears. She was right. I did love Dre more than I loved myself. The sad part was I didn't know any other way. But as she used to say, this too shall pass. D'Andre Mack was about to feel my wrath.

Chapter 15
ALEXUS

"Let me go, Dre!" I screamed as he pulled me back into the room by my shirt.

Dre was back on his bullshit and I was sick of it. We had been arguing all morning about me wanting to go to the mall with Jada. He had a problem whenever I wanted to go somewhere and it always ended with us fighting.

I had him thinking that I was with Jada most of the time, but I had been spending all of my free time with Tyree. He and I were getting closer and I was really starting to like him a lot. I know he was feeling me just as much since he was always on me about leaving Dre to be with him. I still loved Dre, but leaving him to be with Tyree was sounding like a damn good idea.

"You're not going anywhere. Your ass is lying. Always talking about you with Jada!" Dre yelled pulling me from my thoughts.

"Just let me go. You wrong for doing this shit while your kids are here," I yelled.

Dre's kids had been here for the past three days. I didn't have a problem with that because they were good kids, but they were not my responsibility. I wasn't staying inside all day playing mama to this nigga and his children. He was happy as long as I was in the house up under his ass all day.

When I left this time, I was staying away for a few days. I needed some time away from all this madness. I had enough clothes at my sister's house to last me for a while. I would buy whatever I didn't have.

My biggest problem was not having a car. Dre always said he was going to buy me one, but I knew that would never happen. He was content with being the one to drop me off and pick me up from my destination. That was only so he could keep tabs on me. I had enough money saved up to buy me a nice car and I wouldn't have to pay a note on it. I never really spent the money that Dre gave me so that was something that I really needed to consider.

"If you wanted to go shopping that's all you had to say. I could've gone to the mall with you," Dre said.

"Why do I have to go everywhere with you?" I asked. "I like to spend time with my friends sometimes too. And you not my damn daddy so I don't have to ask your permission to go nowhere." I was getting pissed off with this back and forth with his ass.

"Look, I know I'm not your daddy, but you gon' respect me like I respect you. I don't walk out that door without telling you where I'm going."

"I told you I'm going shopping with Jada. What else you need to know?" I asked.

"Yeah, just like last time when that nigga Malik went with y'all," Dre said sarcastically.

"You play all kind of games with your lying ass."

"Nigga, you're the liar. I'm not the one that's married and cheating," I yelled.

"Yeah, cheating with your ass so you can miss me with that married shit," he retorted.

"Whatever Dre. Jada is already on her way and I'm not even dressed." I couldn't wait to get the hell out of there.

"I don't give a fuck! You better call her and tell her you not going," he yelled.

That wasn't happening. I don't care if I left with a black eye and a busted lip, I was leaving. I didn't answer because I knew it would only make matters worse. I proceeded to put my clothes on as if I didn't hear what he said.

"Think I'm playing if you want to," Dre said standing by the bedroom door.

I still didn't answer. I knew he was just looking for a reason to go off on me. If I had to fight my way out then so be it. He was so busy worrying about me; he didn't know what the hell his kids were doing on the other side of the closed door.

When I was done getting dressed, I sat at the foot of the bed, awaiting Jada's call, while Dre was still holding down his spot by the door staring at me. My phone beeped telling me that I had a text message. It was Jada saying that she was on her way and would call when she was out front. Dre and I continued to have a stare down, both refusing to back off.

"I can't see you doing all of this just to go to the mall with Jada. It's more to the story than that," Dre said breaking the silence.

"There's nothing more to the story. You're just too insecure. You are the biggest cheater I know, but you can't take being cheated on," I replied. I regretted making the statement as soon as it left my mouth, but it was too late to take it back. Dre rushed over to me with fire in his eyes.

"So you're admitting the shit! You got somebody else?" he yelled while pulling my hair.

I was so tired of fighting, but I was nobody's punching bag so I had to fight back. I put my designer fingernails to good use and clawed at his face and arms in an attempt to free my hair from his grip.

When that didn't work, I started swinging on him like my life depended on it. He was much taller and stronger than I was, but none of that mattered to me at the moment.

I heard my phone ringing, but there was no way that I could've answered it. Dre and I were fighting like we were in a boxing ring and tearing the house apart in the process. I heard banging on the bedroom door before Dre's oldest daughter ran into the room.

"Daddy, stop!" she cried while tugging at his shirt. I felt so bad for her, but it was her punk ass daddy's fault that all of this was happening.

"Go back in the living room and close the door," Dre yelled out of breath.

"No Daddy. Stop fighting Alexus," she continued to cry. I was still swinging, trying to free myself from the position he had me in on the bed.

Just then, Jada burst through the door with the other kids right behind her.

"What the hell are y'all doing? Dre get off of her!" Jada yelled.

"Mind your fucking business, Jada," he barked at my friend.

"My friend is my business nigga. You doing too much in front of these kids," Jada snapped. We looked up and saw his children crying. Dre got up off of me and went to comfort them. I used that as my opportunity to get the hell out of there. I got up and grabbed my phone and purse, preparing to leave with my friend. I know my hair was a mess, but I didn't care. I just needed to get out of that house.

"Alexus!" Dre yelled as Jada and I made a mad dash for the front door.

I ignored him and kept going. Once we got in the car, I broke down crying, while begging Jada to pull off. Apparently, she was calling my phone, but I didn't answer. When she knocked on the door, Dre's kids let her in and she heard all of the commotion. It was a good thing she came when she did or we would have still been fighting.

"You OK?" Jada asked me softly.

"I'll be alright," I replied. I wasn't so sure about that, but I didn't want her to worry.

"It's gonna be hard for you to leave him and I hope you know that. His ass is obsessed," Jada laughed.

I know she was trying to lighten up the mood, but that only made me feel worse because it was true. Dre had never acted this way before. This was all new to me and I was scared.

"We just need some time apart," I replied lowly. I don't know if I was trying to convince her or myself.

"I just want you to be careful. Don't underestimate him Lex," Jada said with concern in her voice. I knew she was right, but I didn't think Dre would ever hurt me. At least I hope not. One thing was for sure, something had to change and fast. I fixed my hair in the mirror as I reached for my ringing phone. A smile instantly appeared on my face when I saw who was calling.

"Hey Boo," I cooed into the phone feeling like a kid at Christmas. Jada and I looked at each other and exchanged smiles. My day was going from shit to sugar and I had Tyree Taylor to thank for that.

Chapter 16
D'ANDRE

I was stressed the fuck out. Alexus had been gone for three days now and I was losing it. I know I was wrong for always putting my hands on her, but for some reason, she always had a way of bringing out the beast in me. I hated showing my emotions, but I couldn't hide it when it came to her.Eric always laughed at me, saying I was pussy whipped. I never denied it because I couldn't. It was no secret that she had me wide open. Even though I did my thing with other broads from time to time, Alexus would always have my heart. It was killing me to be away from her this long.

I called her phone every five minutes, but she sent all of my calls straight to voicemail. She was back in school so I tried driving around there to see if I saw her. I didn't know where any of her classes were. I usually dropped her off up front and she would disappear into the building. The University was so big; she could have entered from anywhere. They had a million entrances and exits and I didn't have a clue as to where I should start.

She was never at Jada's house because I went there damn near every hour just to see if she would show up.Eric went to her sister's and her mama's house to ask them if they saw her, but they both said no. They didn't know that Eric was my bother and that was a good thing. Alexus's entire family hated me so they would've been more than happy to hide her out. That was cool with me because I was with her and not her family.

I didn't know where her feminine ass brother lived so I couldn't go to his crib. I was public enemy number one to him, but he wasn't dumb enough to step to me. She was always with Jada so I didn't know of any other friends that she could be staying with. My gut was telling me that another man was in the picture. I just refused to believe it.

My mama and my grandmother kept telling me that she was going to be the one to break my heart, but I couldn't accept that as my fate. I was always the one who always did the heartbreaking. I didn't like the way I was feeling at all. My appetite was fucked up so I barely ate. If I slept, it was only for an hour or two, then I was back up stressing about my problems.

My kids had been calling me like crazy about taking them to the skating rink, but I wasn't in the mood to do much of anything lately. I felt bad because I hadn't seen them since all of this happened and I promised them that we could go somewhere. I didn't want them to suffer because of what I was going through.

I looked down at my ringing phone and frowned when I saw that it was Cherika calling. That bitch been blowing up my phone ever since she found out Alexus left. I knew my kids would tell her what happened, but I didn't give a damn. I still didn't want her trifling ass any more.

"Yeah," I answered sounding annoyed.

"What's wrong with you sounding all depressed?" She was enjoying this shit a little too much for me.

"What you want, Cherika?" I snapped.

"Your kids keep asking me if you're coming to get them today. I thought y'all were going to the skating rink," she replied.

"I don't know yet," I sighed. "Tell them we might go tomorrow."

"You have been saying that for the past three days Dre. It's not fair that they have to suffer because you and her having problems!" Cherika yelled.

"First of all, you better watch who the fuck you hollering at! I got a lot of shit to do today so I don't know if I'll be able to go. Tell them we'll go tomorrow and they can spend the night with me," I said, trying to shut her up. Besides, I needed a distraction to keep my mind off of my troubles.

"Ok. I'll let them know so they can stop bothering me about it."

Knowing Cherika, she was probably the only one worried about it. She would use my kids as an excuse to get me over there. I noticed she would always have on some boy shorts or a little ass dress whenever I went to pick up my kids. She even offered to give me head on a few occasions. I was always tempted, but I never took the bait.

"Alright Cherika, tell them I'll be there sometime tomorrow. I'll holler later," I said as I hung up the phone and continued watching TV.

Four days later and it had officially been a week since Alexus left. I was done playing these childish ass games. My mission was to find her so we could at least talk. It shouldn't have been this damn hard to do. I dropped my children off at home and was now sitting outside of Alexus's school once again. I wanted to see if I could ask some of the other students if they knew her. It was kind of empty in front of the school so I assumed everyone was in class. I spotted a tall chick with a backpack on coming my way so I knew she was a student.

"Excuse me," I said as I approached her.

"Yes," she said with a slight attitude. Her hands were on her hips and I knew right from the start that she was a bitch.

"You know a girl named Alexus Bailey that goes to this school?" I asked her.

"No, and I if I did I wouldn't tell you nothing. I don't even know you," she snapped. I was just about to go off on her ugly ass when another chick stepped up and started talking.

"You're talking about Alexus with the long hair and the blonde highlights?" she asked. The other bitch walked off and it was a good thing that she did.

"Yeah, you know her?" I asked.

"If we talking about the same girl, we have a class together," she replied.

"Let me show you her picture," I said as I pulled out my phone. I scrolled through some of my pictures until I found one of Alexus.

"Yeah, that's her. We have our lab lecture at the same time, but we don't go back until Monday," she said. I was a little upset being that today was only Thursday, but at least I was making progress.

"If I give you my number, can you call me when you see her?" I was desperate at this point. She looked like she was hesitant until I pulled a knot of money from my front pocket.

"I got you so don't worry about that," I told her.

"Yeah, I can do that for you," she replied as she eyed my stash. I peeled off three hundred dollar bills and handed them over to her. I wrote my number on the notebook that she handed me.

"Where is the class?" I asked her. The school was big as hell so I didn't know where nothing was located.

"It's in room 107 in building fourteen," she replied.

"Alright, but what's your name?" I asked. I gave this heifer my money and didn't know a damn thing about her.

"My name is Nicole," she replied.

"Alright Nicole; you got my money so make sure you use my number. Don't play any games," I warned her.

"I'm not into playing games. As soon as I see her, I'm going to call you. Is that your girlfriend or something?" she asked me.

"My name is Dre. I'll be waiting to hear from you," I replied, ignoring her question.

"I hope you're not trying to kill her or anything," she yelled as I got in my truck. She was a dumb bitch. Like I would give her my name and number if I was trying to kill somebody. I ignored her once again as I pulled out of the parking lot. As soon as I pulled off, my phone started ringing, displaying Cherika's number. I didn't know what she could have wanted since I just left her house an hour ago.

"What Cherika?" I said into my truck's speakerphone.

"Was Lil Dre feeling bad when he was with you?" she asked.

"No. He didn't say he was feeling bad. Why?"

"He has a fever and he said his stomach hurts," she replied.

"Well give him some Tylenol or something," I said.

"I don't have any in here. Can you pick some up for me?" she asked.

This was the shit I was talking about. With four kids in the house, she should have had any and everything they needed. Alexus even had medicine for them at our house and that wasn't even her kids.

"Yeah, alright, Cherika. I'll be there in a minute," I said, disconnecting the call. I made a U-turn in the middle of the street and headed back in the direction of the drug store.

I used my key to enter Cherika's house and found her and Lil Dre lying on the sofa. When my son saw me, he reached for me to pick him up. He put his head on my shoulder and I felt the warmth coming from his entire body. I sat him down at a bar stool in the kitchen and started opening up the medicine that I just purchased for him.

"I got you some soup and crackers lil man. You have to eat something before you take this medicine," I told my son. I warmed his food and watched him eat as much as he could. When he was done, I gave his some Tylenol and carried him upstairs to his room. I wiped him down with a cold towel and put his pajamas on him. I had been in his room tending to him for over an hour, when Cherika decided to come upstairs.

"How is he feeling?" she asked. I ignored her and continued watching TV. My son was falling asleep and I didn't want to leave until he did.

"Is he feeling any better?" Cherika asked again.

"Look, I been up here with him for almost two hours and you didn't think to come check on him then, so don't come asking me no questions now. He's straight!" I yelled.

"Damn, I was just asking," she said.

"I knew you had him, that's why I didn't come up here," she said as she left out of the room. She was sad. I bet if I was sick, she would have waited on me hand and foot, but she couldn't do the same with her own child.

Once I made sure Lil Dre was asleep, I went to check on my other kids. They were sleeping as well. I walked down the hall in search of Cherika to make sure she gave my son some more medicine in a few hours. I found her in her room wearing nothing but a t-shirt and underwear. I can't lie, she was still fine as hell with her flawless chocolate skin and round ass, but she just wasn't Alexus. I was in love with another woman and my marriage was over because of that fact.

"I'm leaving. Make sure you give him some more medicine before you go to bed. He's sleep so you might have to wake him up," I said from the doorway of her bedroom.

She got up from the bed, sauntered over to me, and pulled me into the room by my arm. Before I could protest, she dropped to her knees and started unbuckling my pants. Any other time I would have slapped the shit out her for pulling a stunt like this, but today was her lucky day. Alexus had been MIA for a week. Me and my man down there were in need of some attention. I closed and locked the door just in case one my kids decided to barge in.

"Damn," was all I could utter as Cherika took me into her mouth and started sucking the life out of me.

After a few minutes, I grabbed the back of her head and pumped faster and harder in her mouth. I heard her gagging as I touched the back of her throat, but I was in a zone and I couldn't stop. I felt my release building up and I was trying to reach the finish line. All of a sudden, Cherika pulled back and stood to her feet. She turned around and bent down, grabbing her ankles. I was too weak to stop her as she guided my hardness into her opening. She wasn't as tight as Alexus, but after having four kids, that was no surprise. We hadn't had sex in a while and I hadn't realized how much I missed it until now. Cherika was a freak in every sense of the word. Nothing was off limits to her in the bedroom. I grabbed her hips and went to work as she tried to keep her balance so she wouldn't fall.

"Damn Dre!" she yelled as I pulled her hair, backing her up into me. I hope she didn't think we were making love. We were straight up fucking.

I felt my release building again, but this time Cherika didn't move. I gripped her hair tighter as I came hard, making both of our bodies shake in the process. I was drained, but Cherika was just getting started. She got up and pushed me back into a chair. My pants were still around my ankles so she removed them and my underwear, leaving me with nothing but my shirt. She got down on her knees and started sucking me until I was hard again. When she was satisfied, she stood up and lowered herself onto my hardness once again. I held her hip firmly in place as she bounced up and down to her own rhythm, never missing a beat. I don't know why, but I had a feeling that I was making a huge mistake.

I woke up the next day feeling hung-over. I adjusted my eyes to the brightness of the room and then it hit me. I was still in Cherika's bed. I looked over at the clock on the nightstand and realized it was after one in the afternoon. My mind replayed the events from the night before and I started to panic. Cherika and I went at it for about three hours and I didn't use protection one time. What the fuck was I thinking about? I got up and went to the bathroom to relieve my bladder. When I got back in the room, Cherika was coming in with a tray of food in her hand.

"Good morning," she said happily. "I made you some breakfast."

She sat the tray down and my mouth started watering. She made me a huge steak, breakfast potatoes, and an omelet. I knew it was good since Cherika could burn in the kitchen. I really didn't know if Alexus could cook because I always took her out to eat.

"Thanks," I said dryly.

"What's wrong?" she asked with concern in her voice.

"Nothing, I'm good," I lied. I didn't want her to think that what happened between us last night meant something because it didn't. It was just sex. I needed it and from the way she reacted, she needed it too.

"Ok, well I'll come back when I think you're done," she said as she left. I ate my food and watched TV, deep in thought. I know I made a mistake by going backwards with Cherika, but fuck it, I couldn't take it back. After I ate, I gathered up my dishes and took everything downstairs. My kids were on the sofa watching TV, fully dressed.

"Daddy can we go somewhere today?" My daughter Denim yelled.

"Where you trying to go?" I asked smiling down at her.

"We can go to the zoo," she replied.

"Alright, I need to go home and take a shower first. I need some fresh clothes."

"How you feeling lil man?" I asked Lil Dre.

"I feel good," he replied smiling.

"You know you still have clothes here right?" Cherika asked me. I just looked at her. I knew what she was doing. I guess she thought that if I left, I wouldn't come back.

"Daddy, you can take a shower and change clothes here," Denim said.

I just shook my head as I headed upstairs for the shower. Cherika knew how to play the game when it came down to my kids. It was sad that she would stoop so low, but that's just the way she was.

Once I took my shower and got dressed, I grabbed my keys and went downstairs. Cherika and the kids were scattered around the living room doing different things.

"Mama is coming with us," Denim announced as I walked in. I stopped in my tracks when she said that. This bitch was doing too much now. I guess she saw the look on my face because she spoke up. "They wanted both of us to bring them so I told them I'll go with y'all." I wasn't in the mood to argue and my kids had seen too much of that already.

"That's cool," I replied. I made a mental note to check her ass about that later on.

Monday evening found me in Cherika's bed once again. Actually, I never left. I had been there since Thursday when I went to bring my son the medicine. Cherika and I were still having sex like crazy, but I made sure to strap up every time. I made up my mind that I was going back home today if I caught up with Alexus or not. I could tell that Cherika was getting use to the idea of me being there and I couldn't have that. I never lied to her about what it was. I kept telling her that we were not back together and I meant that. Every time I made plans to do something with my kids, she somehow included herself in it. She really wanted us to be a family again, but I couldn't do that as long as my heart belonged to somebody else.

My phone started ringing, snapping me from my thoughts. I didn't recognize the number so I sent it straight to voice mail. It started ringing again displaying the same number, but I still didn't answer. After the fourth time, I decided to pick up to see who was blowing up my line.

"Yeah," I yelled into the phone.

"Is this Dre?" A female voiced asked. I tried to remember if I had met anybody in the past few weeks, but nobody came to mind. Not too many females had my number so I didn't know who the hell this could be.

"Why, who is this?" I replied.

"This is Nicole. You told me to call you if I saw Alexus," she said sounding nervous. I instantly perked up when she mentioned Alexus's name.

"Yeah Nicole, what's up?"

"Well she's in class right now, but you better hurry up. We have an exam and we can leave as soon as we're done. I don't know how long she's going to be here," she whispered.

"I'm on my way. good looking out," I said before hanging up. I forgot all about shorty calling me, but I was happy that she did. I jumped up and put my shoes, shirt and hat back on. I took the steps two at a time trying to get to my truck.

"Where you going?" Cherika asked me from the kitchen.

"I'm out. Tell the kids I'll see them later," I replied hurriedly.

"You don't want to eat before you leave?" she yelled out the door.

"No," I replied as I jumped in my truck and pulled off.

I felt bad because I knew she went through a lot of trouble to cook my favorite meal, but there was no way I was staying to eat it. I needed to talk to my baby and get us back on track. Cherika did a good job of keeping me occupied in the bedroom, but that wasn't enough to heal my broken heart. I needed Alexus like I needed air to breathe. I was going to get my oxygen back.

Chapter 17

ALEXUS

I had just finished taking my exam and I was more than happy. I studied from sun up to sun down to make sure I got a good grade. My mind was all over the place lately. It had been a little over a week since I saw or talked to Dre. I would be lying if I said I didn't miss him, but we needed this time apart. I stayed with my sister the first night, but I spent most of my time with Tyree. He had a huge house in the Lakeview area of New Orleans that I fell in love with it.

Ayanna was still picking me up from class just in case Dre ever showed up. He didn't know where any of my classes were, but that never stopped him before. Ayanna told me that somebody came to her and my mama's house looking for me a few days ago. Judging from the description she gave, I knew it was Dre's brother Eric. I knew that would be the first place he looked. Jada lost count of the numerous times he came to her house. He didn't know where my brother lived so that would be my alibi if it ever came down to it.

My sister sent me a text letting me know that she was almost there. I gathered my things and said my goodbyes to a few other students that I was cool with. I walked outside and my heart dropped at the sight before me. Dre was leaning on his truck looking right at me. I wanted to run, but it was too late for all of that. Besides, that would have been childish of me to run when he already saw me. He started walking towards me, but I was frozen in place.

"Hey," he said as he came up close to me.

"Hey," I replied. There was an awkward silence between us as we stared at each other. I don't know why this felt so weird, but it did.

"Can we talk?" he asked. I was just about to respond when Ayanna pulled up. She jumped out of her car with fire in her eyes when she saw Dre.

"You alright, Lex," she asked me as she approached us.

"Yeah, she's alright," Dre said with an attitude before I had a chance to respond.

"I'm not talking to you. She can answer for herself," Ayanna yelled.

"Like I said; she's good!" Dre yelled back. He and Ayanna hated each other with a passion. I had to intervene before things got out of hand.

"I'm good, Ayanna," I told my sister. She just stood there looking like she didn't believe me.

"We need to talk Lex. I'll bring you home when we're done," Dre said while looking at me.

I knew that was a lie. There was no way in hell he would bring me anywhere else but the condo if I got in that truck with him. Ayanna must have been reading my mind because she said what I was thinking.

"You know he's lying, Alexus. He gon' bring you right to his house and beg like the dog he is," Ayanna spat.

"Fuck you Ayanna. You a hater just like the rest of your family. You know she don't want for nothing as long as she with me and you hate that shit," Dre said to my sister. This was getting out of hand, so I decided to end it before it did.

"Dre stop. Go get in the truck and let me talk to my sister," I said with pleading eyes. He looked hesitant so I gave him my backpack and purse to assure him that I was leaving with him.

"You are so stupid," Ayanna said as soon as Dre walked off.

"He got you right where he wants you. You know he's not leaving his wife for you. You got a good man that's really feeling you and you keep wasting your time on his dog ass." I loved my sister, but sometimes she went too far.

"First of all I'm grown. I didn't say that we were getting back together, but if we do, that's my business. We are going to talk and that's all." I walked off after I said what I had to say, but I wasn't done. I turned around and left my sister with a few parting words.

"And just for the record, he already left his wife," I said as I hopped in the truck with Dre.

Ayanna was always so critical of me and my relationships, but she couldn't keep a man to save her life. None of her children's fathers stuck around past a year so she could never give me any advice.

Dre grabbed my hand as we drove down the highway, but I snatched it back. I didn't want him to think that everything was all good between us. We had a lot to talk about and some changes had to be made.

"I know I fucked up Lex and I know you still mad with me, but I promise I'll do anything to make it right between us," Dre said.

Usually I would fall for his lines and we would hit the sheets soon after, but today was not that day. He made a lot of promises when he wanted me back. Things were different for me now. I had somebody that I was developing strong feelings for.

Tyree and I were never intimate, but we bonded on a deeper level than me and Dre did. I wasn't ready to give up on the possibility of us being together. I still had a lot of love for Dre, but I don't think it was enough for us to stay together. He would never let me be happy with anyone else so leaving him was going to be hard.

"Dre, you always say what you think I want to hear, but you never make good on any of your promises," I said.

"I just feel like you suffocate me sometimes." I needed him to give me some space. I was afraid to leave the house most of time because he would have a fit.

"I know that baby, but I'm trying," he said.

"No you're not," I said cutting him off. He didn't respond because he knew it was true. He was jealous, insecure, and possessive and lately he had a problem keeping his hands to himself.

"I'm tired of fighting with you, Dre. I just think we need to go our separate ways," I said while looking away. I could feel him staring at me as we pulled up to the condo, but I wasn't backing down this time. I really wanted this to be over between us.

"I can't do that Alexus. If it was that easy to let you go, I would have done it a long time ago. Maybe we need to talk to somebody about our problems."

"Dre, we can't go to counseling!" I yelled. "We are not married. You trying to make a relationship work with your side chick and there is no counseling for that."

"I wish you stop with that side chick stuff. I hate when you say that shit," he replied annoyed.

We got out of the car and went into the house. I sat on the sofa clutching my purse, while Dre sat on the arm of the love seat.

"You got somebody else, Alexus?" Dre asked me out of the blue.

I hated when he did shit like that. He made me nervous because I thought he already knew something and was trying to catch me in a lie.

"I'm not messing with nobody Dre," I lied.

"I asked you that before and you lied to me "he replied.

"Well I'm not lying to you now," I said with an attitude. He got up and sat next to me on the sofa, grabbing my hand.

"Look, I know we got a lot of shit going on between us, but we need to figure out a way to make this work. We're not going our separate ways so that's not an option. Don't even bring that up again," Dre said.

"Just tell me what you need me to do and I'll do it."

I hated myself for falling for his lines again, but that's exactly what I was doing. I don't know what kind of hold this man had on me, but I couldn't break free.

"Talk to me, Lex," Dre said, pulling me on his lap. "You can't keep running away from all of your problems. That's not solving anything."

He was right, but that was the only way I knew how to deal with my problems. I was always pacified so I didn't know any other way to be.

"I just don't think this is going to work Dre," I finally said.

"You keep saying that, but why don't you think it's going to work?" he asked.

"I have a million reasons why. You hate for me to go anywhere without you. You can't control your temper. You can't keep your hands to yourself. I can go on and on, but it won't change anything," I said out of breath.

"You right, but at the same time you're real sneaky Alexus. You do a lot of shit that I don't know about. That's why I go off when I do find out because I always ask you to tell me the truth."

He was right again, but how do you tell a crazy man that you're cheating on him. I was far from stupid.

"I know you're young and I have to give you some space. I'm willing to do that, but you have to be honest with me about where you go and who you go with."

"This all sounds good Dre, but after a while you'll be back to your old self again."

"No I won't baby, I promise. You have to at least give me a chance to show you. Please," he begged.

He sounded so sincere and my heart melted with every word he spoke. As crazy as it was, I really believed him. I just didn't want him to think that I was giving in too fast.

"Baby please, I'm begging you to give us another chance. I love you too much to live without you," Dre said while kissing my neck.

I don't know if it was his sweet words or his sweet kisses, but I was all in. no more talking was needed when he picked me up and carried me to our bedroom. When he laid me down on the bed, the look in his eyes told me how much he really loved me without a doubt. Dre did things to my body that night that he's never done before. Even still, I couldn't get Tyree off of my mind.

I didn't know if I was making the right decision or not, but I decided to ride the wave until I crashed.

Chapter 18

CHERIKA

Almost two months had gone by and I hadn't seen or heard from Dre since he left my house that Monday night and once again, I felt like a damn fool. I tried to do everything right while he was there and I really thought we were making progress. I cooked a hot meal every day and made sure that the house was cleaned from top to bottom. He was served breakfast in bed every morning while I tended to his sexual needs every night. Before then, Dre and I hadn't had sex in months so I was enjoying every minute of it.

My daughter told me that Alexus was back at home so I knew that she was the reason for him pulling a disappearing act. I guess he didn't want to see me because he sent Eric over to get the kids when he wanted to spend time with them. All of my calls went straight to voicemail so I assumed he had my number blocked. My weight was down again since I was too depressed to eat much of anything. Lately, I always seemed to be the one to get the short end of the stick when it came to my so called husband. Even still, I was not ready to give up on Dre and my marriage.

I was on my way to Santa Fe Bar and Grill in Uptown New Orleans to meet my sisters for drinks. They were pissed with me because they felt like I put them on the back burner when I thought Dre and I were getting back together. It was true, but I would never tell them that. Dre and my sisters didn't get along so I stopped answering the phone for them when he was there.

When Charde came over unannounced one day, I didn't let her in. I didn't want to risk Dre leaving under any circumstances so I met her outside and talked to her on the porch. It took me over a month of apologizing to get them to meet with me today. I already lost Dre; I couldn't lose my sister's too. That would kill me for sure.

When I pulled up, I saw that Cherice was still sitting in her car so I parked right next to her. Charde pulled up a few seconds after I did and parked next to me. We all exited our cars and made our way to our usual seats on the patio.

"Hey ladies," I spoke as we took our seats.

"Hey," they both said dryly. I knew they were still pissed and they had every reason to be. I pretty much said "fuck you" to them both when I thought Dre and I were getting back together. They didn't deserve that when all they ever did was try to help me.

"Look y'all, I know I messed up and I know y'all are still pissed with me, but from the bottom of my heart, I apologize." I said sincerely. I really was sorry for the way that I treated them. They both nodded their heads, but they still didn't say anything. I really needed them to forgive me and I would do anything to make it happen.

"Please forgive me," I begged with tears in my eyes.

"I forgive you and you know I love you, but you really need to get yourself together, Rika,"Cherice said.

"I'm trying Cherice, I really am, but it's hard," I said as the tears fell from my eyes.

"It's only as hard as you make it," Cherice replied.

"You made Dre your whole life and now you feel like you can't live without him. You need to think about your children too."Charde still hadn't said anything since we sat down. I knew she would be a tough shell to crack. She was the more vocal and outspoken out of the two of them.

"You're starting to lose weight again and everything," Cherice said.

"I know I am. My appetite is all messed up," I cried.

"Cherika, you need to stop all this shit," Charde said breaking her silence.

"Dre is a dog, plain and simple. Don't you think for a minute that he won't do her the same thing he's doing to you? That's just the way he is. You are a pretty girl and you can have any man you want. You just too hung up on his ass to move on." I knew she was right, but I didn't know how to move on and I really didn't want to try.

"I know that Charde, but I want a family. That means my husband and children under the same roof," I said.

"Girl, please!" Charde said while standing to her feet.

"I try to keep quiet sometimes, but you need to hear the truth without us always sugarcoating it for you. You are not the only woman that is not with the father of her kids and you won't be the first to get a divorce either. He's running around treating that bitch like she's royalty or something while you sitting at home crying about it. He treats her better than he treats you and you're his wife. You need to stop making a fool of yourself behind a man who clearly does not want you! Fuck D'Andre Mack!" she yelled.

If I never knew how my sisters felt before, I damn sure knew now. If that was how they saw me, I couldn't even imagine what everybody else saw. I couldn't hold it in anymore. I broke down and cried as the truth of my sisters' words hit me like a closed fist. Everything she said was true. My husband didn't love me anymore and I had to live with that. I would have to pray for strength because giving up on Dre and my marriage would be the hardest thing in the world for me to do, but I had to at least try. Both of my sisters rushed over to console me as I literally cried my heart out. I needed to get my life back on track fast.

"Y'all are right," I finally told them while drying my tears. Something had to change starting with me.

"Whaaaat!" Charde laughed. "I must be hearing things. You never agree with nothing we say about Dre."

She was right again. I was so defensive when somebody said something that I didn't want to hear.

"No boo, you're not hearing things. I have to get it together for me and my kids. I know it won't happen overnight, but I have to try," I replied.

"That's what's up," Cherice said smiling. "Now that all of that is out of the way, let's get some food and drinks in our system."

We called our waiter and placed our food and drink orders as we continued to talk and enjoy each other's company.

After we left Santa Fe, my sisters followed me home to drop off me and Charde's car. Cherice wanted to hit up the mall and we were more than happy to accompany her. My kids were with Dre and I didn't want to be home by myself. I was still feeling down so I was hoping some retail therapy would help to lift my spirits. I know I told them that I would try to get over Dre, but I was having second thoughts already. Just the thought of losing him to another woman sickened me to no end. It was true that I would have no problem finding another man, but Dre was the only man I wanted. It would take some time and maybe a little scheming, but I was getting my husband back one way or another. However, I did it would just be my little secret.

When we got to the mall, all of us wanted to hit up Victoria's Secret to get us some perfume and lotion. I was going crazy picking up damn near everything I saw. I was spending the money that Dre had given me for our kids, but I didn't care. He could afford to replace it. He was spending mad money on Alexus. She stayed fly and never worked a day in her young life.

I grabbed all of my items and made my way to the register. My sisters were waiting for me since they were already done. I didn't know who this bitch was in front of the line, but she was buying up the whole damn store. She was taking forever and this was the only register open.

"Y'all need to open up another register," Charde yelled as she walked up and stood next to me.

"Damn right," I co-signed getting impatient.

Just then, I saw Alexus's friend Jada walk up and take some of the bags that the cashier had put to the side. I would know her fake ass from anywhere. It was no secret that she and Alexus were thick as thieves so that bitch couldn't be too far behind.

"That's Alexus's friend," I said to Charde, nodding my head in Jada's direction. We both started looking around to see if we could spot her in there too.

"Look, don't come in this mall with all that bullshit! I'm not trying to go to jail cause y'all in here fighting," Cherice said.

Cherice was always the voice of reason, but I wasn't trying to hear that peacemaker shit today. Jada started walking in our direction followed by Alexus. She was rocking blonde highlights now so that was why I didn't recognize her when she was at the register.

When I looked at the millions of bags she was carrying, my blood started to boil. This bitch was spending my husband's money like she had his last name and carried his babies.

I couldn't even front, the little bitch was bad. I was far from ugly, but my shape wasn't what it was before. My weight had been up and down over the past few months because Dre had me stressing like crazy. She had flawless skin and her shape would make anybody do a double take when she walked by. I could see why Dre fell for her the way he did. He was a sucker for a pretty face and a fat ass. No matter how much weight I lost, that was the one thing on my body that never went away.

They walked past us and Alexus had a smirk on her face that I wanted to knock off. I couldn't just let her walk past me, so I dropped everything that I was holding and followed them out of the store.

"Cherika, don't start nothing with that girl," Cherice said as she followed close behind me. I ignored her and kept walking behind my targets.

"Something funny hoe," I yelled as I walked up on the both of them.

They both kept walking, but didn't say anything. Alexus was laughing and that only added fuel to the fire. They walked through the food court towards the mall's exit with me hot on their heels.

"Cherika you look like a damn fool following behind that girl. We just talked about this earlier. Leave it alone and lets go," Cherice said.

"Fuck that!" I yelled.

"I want to know what's so funny since she keeps snickering and shit." I know I was making a fool out of myself, but I didn't care. I hated this girl with a passion. If she had come into the picture, my family would be intact. At least that's the way I saw it. I was just about to stop following them when they stopped at Dre's car. My face dropped and I got mad all over again. This was the same car that he refused to let me drive when we were together. They started loading their bags into the trunk, completely ignoring me and my sisters. That only made things worse.

"Scary ass," Charde said as we continued to stand there.

Alexus was far from scary and I knew that first hand, but for some reason, she didn't feel the need to entertain us today. I guess she had enough of us because she finally spoke up.

"Bitch, I'm far from scary. Just ask your sister," she said to Charde.

I was already in attack mode so her word sent me right over the edge. I tried to run up on her, but Cherice stopped me before I could. A few people started gathering around us as we screamed and yelled at each other in the parking lot. The mall security was headed towards us so I knew I wouldn't be to get to her once they came. Charde and Alexus were still screaming at each other when security walked up on us. My sister told me about Alexus pushing her when they were at the tattoo shop so I assumed she was still mad about that.

"Bitch you going hard behind a nigga that's not even yours. Maybe it's because you sucking his dick too. Tell your sister how you give her husband head every chance you get. Nasty ass bitch!" Alexus yelled.

My whole world stopped when she said that. I didn't have any more fight left in me. That had to be a lie. Dre and Charde hated each other so there was no way possible they were fooling around. I knew my sister had a ratchet past, but I hope that past didn't include Dre. That would be too much for me to deal with.

"Don't be quiet now. You weren't quiet a minute ago. Tell your sister what the deal is," Alexus continued to yell.

Through it all Charde remained quiet, but her silence spoke volumes as far as I was concerned. I knew my sister better than anyone else did. She was guilty.

"Y'all have to leave or I'm calling the police," the security guard told us.

"Come on y'all," Cherice said. Alexus and Jada got in the car and pulled off as my sisters and I searched the parking lot for Cherice's car.

When we found the car, I stood in front of the door, blocking it so Charde couldn't get in. I wanted some answers and she was going to give them to me.

"Tell me she was lying, Charde," I said while looking in my sister's eyes.

She dropped her head, but didn't respond. I couldn't believe this shit. She was the main one who was always on my back about leaving Dre, but she was the same one who was fucking him behind my back. I hauled off and slapped her across her face. I followed up with a series of punches to her body until Cherice pulled me away. "Cherika stop! Are you crazy?" Cherice yelled pulling me away.

"Let me go! That bitch is the main one bad mouthing my husband, but she go behind my back and sleep with him," I cried.

"I never slept with him, I swear," Charde said crying.

"Oh I forgot, you just sucked his dick," I yelled sarcastically.

It was bad enough that Dre kept hurting me; now my sister was doing the same thing. I didn't know how much more I could take.

"I'm so sorry, Cherika," she cried. "I know I was wrong and I swear it'll never happen again."

"Why would you do it in the first place?" I asked her. I wanted to know what I had done to her that was so bad that she would do me so wrong. I loved my sisters with everything in me. I shared everything with them, but my husband was supposed to be off limits.

"It was a mistake. I don't have an excuse or a reason why it happened, but I am so sorry. Please don't let this come between us," she said crying. How could something like that have gotten past me? It just didn't make sense.

"Tell me the truth, Charde. Did you and Dre ever have sex?" I asked the question, but I was afraid to get the answer.

"No, I swear we never had sex. That was all that happened between us," she said while looking me in my eyes.

I knew she was telling the truth because she made eye contact with me. I really wanted to hate my sister, but I couldn't. I didn't have a big family so we were very close. So many bad things were happening to me lately and I truly believed that I was being punished for my past.

"Let's go y'all. Maybe we can go somewhere and talk," Cherice said.

"Yes. I need a drink," I said as we all piled into the car in route to wherever alcohol was sold.

We ended up at a daiquiri shop in New Orleans East. It wasn't as crowded as it usually was so we decided to go in and get us a table.

Once we got our drinks, we sat at a table in the corner. Charde and I had a long and much needed talk. She explained to me how everything happened. It was no surprise that Dre was the one that approached her. Although I forgave her, I couldn't trust her anymore. She would have to work hard to earn that back. She could have told me when he came at her, but she chose to entertain his advances. This wasn't the first storm we had been through so I knew we would overcome this one as well.

if I could forgive Dre for constantly cheating on me, then I could do the same for my sister. Charde didn't have the best reputation and Dre was a sucker for some good head so it wasn't hard to see how they ended up together. He had a lot of explaining to do as well since he was just as wrong as Charde was.

"I'm ready to bounce. This has been a long ass day," I announced to my sisters, after about three hours of talking and drinking.

"It sure has," Cherice replied. "Let me run to the bathroom before we go." When Cherice got up, Charde used that as an opportunity to talk to me again.

"I know it's gonna take some time to repair our relationship, but I'm willing to do whatever I have to do to regain your trust," she told me, squeezing my hand.

"I know it won't happen overnight, but I just want us to work on it," she continued. I smiled at her and nodded my head, letting her know that I heard everything that she said. Forgiving her was the easy part. I would never be able to trust her around my husband again. There's no telling how long this secret would have been kept if Alexus hadn't said anything. I had many more questions to ask, but I was tired of talking about it for the time being.

After a few minutes, Cherice came running back to the table.

"Guess who I just saw at the polka machine in the back?" Cherice yelled excitedly.

"Who?" Charde and I said simultaneously.

" Keanna's messy ass," she replied.

"Who is she back there with?" I asked standing to my feet.

"I don't know. I saw her when I went to the bathroom. She playing on the machine in back corner. She didn't even see me."

"I'm going back there," I said walking off.

"No. You can't do anything in here. We all going to jail if you do," Cherice said. I knew my sister had a point, but I was itching to get to that hoe.

"Let's just go outside and wait until she comes out," Charde suggested.

"It's almost one and they should be closing soon." That was a good idea. After all, she had to come out sooner or later.

When my sisters and I got outside, I noticed Keanna's car immediately. I guess I wasn't looking for it before so I didn't see it. We got in Cherice's car and pulled up two spaces from where she was parked and waited. My adrenaline was pumping and I couldn't wait to get my hands on Keanna. The whole time she was feeding me info about Dre and Alexus, she turned out to be the one that put them together. Even though it was never confirmed about her doing the DNA test on Troy and Drew, she was guilty until proven innocent. She was the only suspect in my eyes. Nobody else had a motive.

After waiting for about forty-five minutes, we finally saw Keanna coming outside looking down at her phone. As soon as she got close to the car, we jumped out on her ass.

"What's up Keanna?" I asked.

She grabbed her chest as if I scared her, but she appeared to be unfazed by our sudden appearance.

"Girl, you scared the hell out of me. What y'all doing out here?" She asked like everything was all good. I hope this bitch didn't think this was a friendly visit because it was far from that.

"Don't worry about what we doing here. What I want to know is, why would you hook Dre up with somebody else knowing he was married? Then you want act like you were on my side when you were the cause of all this shit happening in the first place." I was waiting for her ass to lie, but I guess she knew it was useless.

"First of all, I didn't have to hook your so called husband up with nobody. He was a hoe when you met him so he was going to cheat regardless. But while we're asking questions, I have a few to ask you," she said while snaking her neck.

"Out of all the niggas in the world, why would you fuck Troy?" She asked.

"Then you did the shit in my house, in my bed all while you were smiling in my face. And on top of all of that, you got pregnant for the nigga and tried to put the baby on my cousin. Yeah, I know all about the DNA test," she said with a smirk on her face.

"Bitch, I guess you do know about it since you were the one who did it," I said.

"I sure did," she replied in a matter of fact tone.

"Dre was gon' leave you for Alexus anyway. I just sped up the process."

I was done talking after she said that. I ran towards her swinging and got a few licks to the side of her face. She dropped everything she was holding and started swinging back. A few people came out of the daiquiri shop to watch what was going on. Keanna quickly got the best of me as she pulled my hair and slung me to the ground. She was about to kick me in my face when my sisters jumped in and started swinging on her.

I got up and joined them as they punched and kicked every part of Keanna's body. She was trying her best to keep up with us, but she was outnumbered. A few minutes passed before two bouncers came outside and broke up the ruckus that we were causing.

"Y'all hoes can't fight. Y'all had to jump me," Keanna yelled as she was being helped up from the ground. "Bitch, don't get mad with me because a youngster took your husband!" she yelled, pissing me off even more.

"Get in y'all ride and leave before I call the police," one of the bouncers said to us.

He didn't have to tell us twice. We rushed over to Cherice's car and burned rubber getting out of the parking lot.

"That ho made me break my nail," I complained as we drove away.

My finger was throbbing and bleeding all at the same time. I knew that this was far from over because Keanna was known for playing dirty. She believed in getting revenge if she felt that somebody had wronged her. I wasn't scary, but I would have to watch my back since I knew I would definitely be on her list.

Chapter 19
KEANNA

I couldn't believe those scary bitches jumped me. I didn't claim to be the best fighter in the world, but I could hold my own when it was one on one. Cherika and her sisters couldn't fight for shit so they were always jumping somebody. I was in my bathroom mirror looking at the damage they had done to my face. I had a small bruise under my left eye and a few scratches, but it was nothing that a little makeup couldn't fix. Since it was three against one, I should have been in far worse shape than I was in. That was how I knew none that of them bitches had hands. It was far from over though. I would make sure I saw each and every one of them again, especially Cherika. I still had a few tricks up my sleeve for her nasty ass.

I walked to my kitchen to fix myself a drink when my phone started ringing. I knew it was Troy because he had been blowing my phone up for the past few days. I kept telling him that I couldn't come up with the money to get him out, but he wasn't trying to hear that. I went to my walk in closet in search of the perfect outfit for later today.

TJ, the owner of the building where I worked, gave me a VIP invitation to the grand opening of the club that he was leasing to his friend. Well he actually gave it to his dad to give to me, but I was still happy that he even thought of me at all. Troy and nobody else was going to ruin my day. I kind of wished TJ would have invited me to go with him, but I would take what I could get for now.

Tonight was going to be the night that I told him how I feel. I was tired of crushing on him from a distance. There was nothing shy about me so I wasn't scared to put my feelings out there. He never mentioned having a girlfriend so that was a good thing. Knowing how good he looked, he was probably a ladies' man just like Dre.

I finally emerged from my closet after settling on a black and gold Juicy Couture halter dress. I had a pair of black stilettos with gold spikes that would be perfect with it. I didn't have that much ass, but I have enough breasts and a flat stomach to make it work. It was after two in the morning, but I still sat at my vanity and put a few flexible rollers in my hair. I wanted everything to be perfect and a curly up-do would be perfect with my chosen outfit. My phone started ringing again right after I put the last roller in my hair and this time I answered.

"Hello," I said trying to sound tired.

"Your ass is not sleeping so you can stop faking," Troy yelled into the phone.

He called me all times of the day and night from a cell phone that one of the guards smuggled in for the inmates.

"It's late, Troy. What do you want?" I asked with an attitude.

"Bitch, you sure been talking reckless since I been locked up huh? I ain't going to be in this bitch forever, remember that," he replied. "What's going on with you trying to get me out of here? These people trying to make me do six months if I don't come up with the bail money."

" I already told you that I can't come up with that kind of money by myself. I'm working a bunch of overtime trying to keep these bills paid."

If I did have the money, I wouldn't have gotten him out anyway. He needed to be in there to detox. I was really feeling TJ so I didn't care if he ever came home.

"So you can't ask anybody in your family to lend you the money? What about Dre? He spends more than that taking that bitch Alexus shopping. I know he got it," Troy said.

He was foul as hell for even asking me to go to Dre for help. Nobody in my family would give me a dime to help him out.

"Well, maybe if you wouldn't have been fucking his wife while he was in jail he probably would have helped you out. And besides, you was the one who stopped fucking with him, not the other way around," I replied sarcastically.

"What! Who said I fucked her? That's a lie," Troy said like I was stupid.

"Ok Troy. Play dumb if you want to. Dre already knows everything. And he knows that Drew is yours too."

"Man you got me fucked up! That lil boy is not mine!" He shouted. I could see he was going to take this lie to his grave so I decided to put a stop to it now.

"Troy I did the test myself so I know that you're Drew's father," I told him. He was quiet for a while and I knew I had him right where I wanted him.

"Baby look, it wasn't even like you think. It only happened one time and I took her to a motel," he lied.

"One time, huh? So y'all never had sex in my bed or on my sofa or my kitchen counters?" I asked him.

"That bitch told you that? She lying Keanna. She just trying to make you leave me," he said trying to convince me.

"Nobody is trying to make me leave you Troy. You're doing a damn good job of that all by yourself," I replied.

"Baby she lying, I promise. I'm not going to lie; I did have sex with her, but not in our house. I wouldn't do you like that," he continued to say.

"I was just a bitch a minute ago, but since you know your ass is busted, I'm baby now. And for your information, Cherika didn't tell me anything. She's a liar, just like you. I have my ways of finding out what I need to know," I said as I hung up on his lying ass.

I turned my ringer off and prepared to take my shower. I had a long day ahead of me and I wanted to be well rested before I met up with TJ. It would have been nice if I had somebody to go with me, but I didn't have many friends and my cousins were still mad with me. They took Cherika's side once they found out that I was the one who tested Drew. I came clean once I saw that all the evidence pointed to me. Nobody ever took the time out to ask me how I felt. After all, it was my man that she slept with and had a baby by. It didn't matter to me one way or another. My goal was to get Dre to leave her and that mission was accomplished.

I looked at my reflection in the mirror and blew a kiss at the bad bitch who stared back at me. My hair and makeup were flawless and the outfit I chose was on point. I was a little nervous about seeing TJ outside of work, but after a few drinks, the butterflies in my stomach would go away. I pulled my car up to the VIP section of the club and waited until the valet came to open my door.

The club was in a nice area on Manhattan Blvd. on the Westbank of New Orleans. The exterior was well lit and the parking was plentiful. Before I walked inside, I popped a mint and sprayed on a little perfume. I wanted to smell as good as I looked. There was no line, so I handed the guy at the door my invite. In return, he gave me a neon green bracelet, allowing me to enter and exit the VIP area with no problems.

When I walked into the club, my entire face dropped as I looked around in awe. The outside looked almost like a lighted warehouse, but the inside was simply amazing. The color scheme was royal blue and silver. There were mirrors surrounding the entire dance floor, allowing dancers to see themselves as they moved around. The floors were made of blue and silver tiles that gave the place and elegant look. A spiraled staircase led the way to the upstairs VIP section so I headed that way. The club was pretty crowded to say it was still early. I bumped into a few people as I made my way to the staircase.

"Hey you," a male voice said from behind me. I turned around and came face to face with Malik. "Hey yourself," I spoke back to him. I guess I never it noticed before, but he was very handsome. I guess he had to be if Alexus dated him. A man had to look a certain way for her to even give them a second look.

"I haven't seen you in a while," he said.

"Yeah, I've been working like crazy," I replied.

"Where's your friend?" Malik asked.

"What friend are you referring to?" I asked.

"Alexus," was his simple reply. If I had been anywhere else, I would have given him a piece of my mind. He was only getting a pass because I was in a good mood.

"That's not my friend. She's just my cousin's girlfriend," I said.

"She should be the last person you're asking about after what happened to you."

I heard about Dre getting some of our cousins to attack Malik and some of his friends at the bar a few months ago. Malik walked away from the brawl with a broken jaw. He was crazy as hell for worrying about Alexus.

"Yeah, but that didn't have nothing to do with her. Your cousin is just crazy," he laughed.

"Yeah, well she's still with his crazy ass so you better keep it moving," I told him as I walked up the stairs. It wasn't as crowded in VIP as it was downstairs. I guess too many people didn't have access. I strolled over to the bar while scanning the small crowd for TJ. I didn't see him so I ordered a watermelon martini. I sat in one of the bar stools while my drink was being prepared. The atmosphere was nice and I could see myself coming here quite often.

"I see you made it," a male voice said from behind. I would recognize that smooth baritone from anywhere. I turned around and smiled up at TJ. To say he looked damn good was an understatement. His eyes were mesmerizing.

"You look nice," he said while looking me over. Nice wasn't exactly the compliment I was going for, but I would take anything coming from him.

"Thanks," I replied. "You look good too." Every time I saw him, he was rocking a fresh pair of Jordans and some jeans. Seeing him in his linen outfit and Cole Haan dress shoes made me want him even more.

"Where are you sitting?" I asked him. I wanted to be wherever he was.

"Nowhere at the moment. I'm waiting on some people to get here before I sit down."

"Oh, you got your lil boo coming to keep you company?" I just threw that out there, but I was hoping that wasn't the case.

"Something like that," he replied to my disappointment.

I really didn't care about whoever she was. I had no problem competing for what I wanted. TJ and I sat around talking and sipping on our drinks. I was trying my best to let him know that I was feeling him without actually saying it. Everything I said seemed to go over his head. Either that or he wasn't interested. Our conversation was flowing until he got a text message and excused himself.

"I'll be right back. I'm going to meet my people outside," he said while getting up. I couldn't wait to see who it was that had him smiling so damn hard. I ordered myself another drink and waited for him to return.

"What you doing here?" I heard a female voice ask.

I looked to the side and saw Jada standing there. She couldn't stand me and the feeling was mutual.

"Keanna?" another female voice said from behind.

Why did Alexus and her flunky pick tonight to be in the same place as me? I conjured up a fake smile and looked her way. My smile faded immediately when I saw TJ with his arms wrapped around her waist. I couldn't believe that this was who he was waiting for. After a few seconds, two other girls, who appeared to be twins, joined us at the bar.

"Damn, y'all know each other?" TJ asked us.

"Yeah. Me, Keanna and Jada went to school together," Alexus replied. I noticed her sneaky ass conveniently left out the part about her being my cousin's girlfriend.

"Oh Ok. Well since I don't need to introduce y'all, Keanna these are my lil sisters, Katina and Katrina," he said. We exchanged pleasantries as everyone placed their drink orders.

"How do you know Tyree?" Alexus asked me. I almost forgot that Tyree was his real name. TJ stood for Tyree, Jr. since that was also his dad's name. Not many people used his real name and everyone in the office called his dad Mr. Tee.

"He owns the building where I work," I replied.

"How do y'all know each other?" I asked her right back.

"He's Jada's cousin. We met at a gathering at his mama's house." That really pissed me off. She had already met his mama and she appeared to be close with his sisters already.

"This is my baby," Tyree said while kissing her neck.

"I'm trying to get her to make this thing official." I wanted to vomit as I watched the two of them hug and kiss like they were newlyweds. This night was definitely not going like I wanted it to go.

We all made our way over to an empty sofa and sat down. I was feeling like the odd one in the crew. Alexus and Tyree were damn near joined at the hip while Jada and her cousins talked amongst each other. Tyree's sisters tried to include me in their conversation, but Jada made it her business to completely ignore me.

"You're staying with me this weekend right?" Tyree asked Alexus.

I almost choked on my drink when he said that. She looked over at me before whispering in his ear. He was smiling like a damn fool. I felt sick to my stomach. I was so sick of her winning at everything. TJ had been on my radar for a while now, but this bitch had to mess it up for me. I now knew how Cherika would feel whenever her name came up. I was starting to hate Alexus just as much as she did.

It wasn't enough that she had one man falling all over her, but she had to have the one I wanted too. I had all kinds of evil thoughts running through my mind, but I settled on one in particular. I only had to make one phone call and Alexus and TJ's weekend would be anything but pleasant. I excused myself from everyone and went to the bathroom. I took a deep breath and calledDre.

Chapter 20
ALEXUS

I was shocked to see Keanna sitting in the VIP section of the club when we got there. It had been a minute since I last talked to her. I know that Dre and his sisters were feeling some kind of way about her doing a DNA test on Drew, but that didn't have anything to do with me. That was their family's business.

I noticed she would sneak peeks at Tyree and me, but I didn't care. I wanted her to run back and tell Dre. That would make everything that much easier for me. As usual, he was ringing my phone off the hook every five minutes. He was probably trying to see when I was coming home. I hated to hurt his feelings, but I had no plans on going home at all this weekend.

Tyree had been begging me for weeks to spend the weekend with him. He was mad when I went back home to Dre so I figured that was the least I could do. He told me he had something special planned for our night and I couldn't wait to see what it was. I had a feeling that he wanted us to take our relationship to the next level sexually and I was more than ready.

We had been kicking it for a few months now, but we never did anything more than kiss. I tried to take it there a few times, but Tyree would always say the timing wasn't right. It didn't matter what he said tonight, it was going down for sure.

"I'll be right back," Tyree said, kissing me on the lips. He was back and forth taking pictures and talking with the club's owner. He wasn't the clubbing type, but since it was his building, he had to be in attendance.

"Girl, Dre is going to kill you," Keanna laughed.

"Fuck Dre!" Jada spoke up before I had a chance to.

"She is grown and if she wants to be with somebody else then so be it."

I knew this conversation was more personal for Jada seeing as how Tyree was her cousin. She saw how happy we made each other and she wanted us to be together. Besides that, she hated Dre and his entire family.

"I'm talking to Alexus," Keanna said to Jada.

"And I'm talking to you," Jada snapped.

Tina and Trina were looking on in shock as the two of them passed words back and forth. They went from talking about me and Dre to talking about each other. I saw that the situation was getting out of hand, so I decided to intervene.

"Ok y'all, let's hit the bar again," I said as I got up from my seat.

I made a mental note to talk to Jada when Keanna wasn't around. I knew how she felt about Keanna, but this was not the time or the place for drama. Tyree didn't deserve to have his night ruined by them fussing and fighting. Jada never acted this way with anyone before so I knew it was serious. She was usually so calm.

Keanna was acting kind of nervous. I noticed that she would get up every so often to use her phone. If she wasn't on it, she was checking it. I wasn't sure what that was all about, but it was pissing Jada off. "That bitch is a snake," she kept saying.

"Something is not right with her," Katrina agreed.

"I'm telling you, Alexus is the only one that can't see she's shady," Jada replied.

"You see how she did Cherika. They were friends, but she hooked you up with Dre. She is cut throat. Don't say I didn't warn you when that bitch crosses you." Jada was going off. I just laughed as they went on and on about something that I didn't even care about. Keanna was not a threat to me at all.

"Guess who's in here," Keanna asked me when she came back to her seat.

"Who?" I asked her.

"Girl, Malik. He asked about you too. I told him that Dre is still crazy and he better keep it moving," she laughed.

I don't know why she insisted on bring Dre's name up all night. He was the last person I wanted to talk about. I kind of felt like she was doing it on purpose, knowing Tyree's sisters were sitting right her with us. It wasn't like it was a secret. Everybody knew that I was with Dre, including Tyree and his family.

"Girl I'm not worrying about Malik, Dre and nobody else for that matter. I'm here with the man that I want to be with," I replied.

I could tell that she didn't like what I said just by the look on her face, but I meant every word. Tyree was like a breath of fresh air. I never realized how unhealthy Dre was for me until I met Tyree. He didn't treat me like a child. We had a lot in common and we got along good. I was starting to fall in love and it scared me.

It wasn't a question of if he felt the same way because I know he did. He told me he was falling in love with me weeks ago. I just needed to get away from Dre and stay away. For some reason he had a hold on me that I couldn't explain. He wasn't going to let me go without a fight and I didn't want to involve Tyree in all of my madness. He told me that he could deal with whatever was thrown at him and I believed that he could. Dre was cut from a different cloth and I knew how he got down.

"So how long have you been talking to Tyree?" Keanna asked.

"Long enough to know she loves me," he said sitting down next to me, laughing. Keanna tried hard, but she failed to mask the envious look on her face. I was starting to take heed to some of the words that Jada spoke.

"I'll be right back," she said getting up from the sofa.

"I think you got a secret crush," I told Tyree.

"Who, Keanna?" he asked.

"Yes, Keanna," Jada said.

"Don't act like you don't know. She has been mean mugging my friend on the slick all night. She about to get her assed whopped if she keep it up." Jada was in rare form tonight.

"Don't start nothing in this man club Jada," Tyree said.

"This is his first night opening the doors." I had to make sure I stayed close to Jada just in case she had other plans.

I had a funny feeling about something and I was ready to go anyway. Being here was important to Tyree so I had to wait until he was ready.

"How long you have to stay here?" I asked him over the music.

"I can leave whenever I'm ready. I just wanted to show my face. You ready to go?" he asked. I hated to say yes, but my first mind was telling me that it was time.

"Yeah, I'm hungry," I replied. I didn't want to tell him about the feeling I was having, so I left it at that. Tyree stood up and grabbed my hand,

"We're about to go y'all, come on," he said to his sisters and Jada. Trina was talking to one of the bartenders and it didn't look like she would be ready anytime soon.

"Y'all go ahead. I know why y'all rushing to get out of here," Jada laughed.

"Hell no, you not staying in here so you and Keanna can shut this man's club down," Tyree told her. "We got her. She'll be alright," Tina said.

"You sure?" I asked Tina.

"Yeah, y'all go ahead. Nobody not trying to be in here fighting like children," Tina said while looking at Jada.

Tyree grabbed my hand and we headed down the staircase. When we got downstairs, it was packed to full capacity. Tyree pulled me close so I wouldn't get lost in the crowd. We were almost to the exit when I felt somebody tapping me on the shoulder. I stopped walking to turn around only to come face to face with Eric. It was as if all the wind was knocked from my body. He looked from me to Tyree, then back at me again.

"What's up Alexus?" Eric said with a smirk on his face.

"Hey," I replied nervously. He was looking at Tyree like he was trying to figure out who he was.

"Is this your boo or something?" Eric asked while still looking at us.

"Or something, nigga. Let's go, Lex," Tyree said while pulling me along.

"Nigga, I wasn't talking to you. Mind your fucking business," Eric said to Tyree.

"Nigga, she is my business," Tyree said standing in front of me.

"You good fam?" One of the bouncers asked Tyree.

"Yeah, I'm straight," he said as we started walking off again.

"We'll see each other again," Eric said to Tyree as we walked out of the club.

My first mind has never let me down. I knew it was a reason for the weird feelings I was having. I was so happy that we were leaving. Knowing Eric, he was telling Dre about me and Tyree at this very moment.

Chapter 21

KEANNA

When I got back to the table, TJ and Alexus were gone. "Where did Lex go?" I asked one of Tyree's sisters.

"She and Tyree left," his sister told me.

"She trying to be alone with her man," Jada said, putting emphasis on the word man.

I couldn't stand that heifer and she knew it. She was always trying to get under my skin. This time it was working. It was killing me to know that Alexus and TJ were together. I had been calling Dre for an hour before he finally picked up. He said he was on his way, but he hadn't showed up yet.

I was wrong for getting him involved, but I was desperate. I wanted TJ and that was the bottom line. I knew that if Dre showed up, he would drag Alexus out of the club and no one was going to stop him. Once that happened, I would be left alone with TJ and I could make my move.

that was supposed to be the plan. I didn't think they would leave so soon. I was pissed with myself, but I was even more pissed with Dre. If he had come when he said he would, they would probably still be here. That wasn't like Dre at all.

Now I was wondering if everything was alright with him. Usually when something involved Alexus, he would drop everything to get there. I grabbed my purse and got up from the sofa, preparing to leave. I looked around the VIP section one last time just to be sure they weren't in there. I walked down the spiral staircase and was met byEric.

"Hey cuz. What you doing in here?" I asked him. I could tell he was pissed, just by the look on his face. He looked at me, but didn't say anything. I knew he wasn't mad with me like his sisters and Dre was, because we still talked regularly.

"You good cousin?" I asked again.

"Man, I don't know who that nigga was that Alexus was with, but he was about to get fucked up!" Eric fumed. I knew he was talking about TJ, but I wondered what could have happened.

"Let's go outside. It's too noisy in here," I told him as I led the way out of the club.

"What happened?" I asked him once we were outside.

"That nigga was in there popping off like he wanted to do something. We gon' see each other again. Believe that." Eric said angrily.

I didn't want to tell him that I knew TJ. He and Dre could be crazy at times and I didn't want anything to happen to Tyree. It wasn't his fault that Alexus was a hoe. He just got caught up with the wrong one. Dre was not about to let her be with somebody else as long as he had breath in his body. I don't know what the hell she did to my cousin, but I hope she never got the chance to do the same to Tyree.

"Dre needs to leave her sneaky ass alone. That hoe got his nose wide open," Eric said. He had to really be mad because he was one of the very few who liked Alexus.

"I saw her upstairs with a dude. I called him and he been said he was on his way, but he never showed up," I told my cousin.

"I called him too, but he never answered," Eric replied.

"He could have stayed with his own wife if he wanted to deal with some bullshit," he said.

"And you right cousin," I cosigned.

"That nigga don't want you to say nothing about her, but she a straight up hoe. I'll tell him to his face and I don't care if he gets mad. At least Cherika waited until he got locked up before she fucked around," Eric said.

"He just need to go back home to his family," I said, but I didn't mean that shit at all. That was the last thing I wanted him to do. If anything, I wanted him to be with Alexus more than ever now. At least that would give me a chance with Tyree.

"Well, I'm about to go. Who did you come here with?"

"I came with some of my friends, but I'm riding back with you. I'll text them and let them know. I don't even feel like partying any more. Then they ruined my damn high," Eric complained. I called the valet over and gave him the ticket to retrieve my car.

Eric was still trying to call Dre, but he still didn't answer. I don't know what the problem was, but something had to be wrong. I could see him not answering for me, but he never ignored Eric's calls. When the valet pulled up with my car, we got in and left out of the parking lot.

"He's still not answering?" I asked Eric as we drove off.

"Nope; I don't know what's up with that dude. You know how he act when somebody tell him something about her. He might be waiting for her to come home so he can beat her ass," Eric said.

"Well according to her and ol' boy's conversation, she's not going home tonight," I replied, repeating what I heard them say.

"What! Dre gon' end up killing her ass," Eric replied.

"I hope my cousin don't get himself in trouble playing around with her ratchet ass," I said. I never knew Alexus to be a hoe, but she had been proving me wrong lately. First, it was Malik and now she was with Tyree. Even after all of that I knew that Dre would never leave her alone. He was forever making excuses for her.

"I hope he don't get in no trouble either," Eric said, breaking my thoughts. He started to say something else when his phone rang.

"This that nigga calling me right now," he said.

"Where you at, man? I have been calling you for a minute." I don't know what Dre was saying, but it couldn't have been good, judging from Eric's face.

Chapter 22
D'ANDRE

After I put my kids to bed, I grabbed my bottle of Patron and my blunt and stretched out on the sofa. Alexus went out with some of her girls so I was on my own for a while. Our relationship seemed kind of off lately. I tried doing everything that I could think of to put a smile on her face, but it never seemed to be enough.

She complained about the smallest shit. She was getting tired of my kids being here so much so I slacked up with their visits. That still didn't work. She always found something else to be mad about. It was crazy that I went out of my way to please her and I had a wife who was willing to do the same for me. I ran after Alexus like Cherika ran after me.

I know I did Cherika wrong, but I just didn't love her any more. It was wrong of me to even spend nights at her house and even worse that I slept with her. In her mind, we were getting back together and I know I led her on. She wanted more from me than I was willing to give. I asked her for a divorce a million times, but she wasn't trying to hear me.

Our entire marriage was doomed from the start. She had me by the balls when I was locked up so I really didn't have a choice. I tried telling her that we'd get married when I got out, but she knew that was a lie. Lately she had been on some stalker shit and I ended up having to restrict her calls because she called me so much. She didn't care what time of the day or night it was, she would ring my phone off the hook. Alexus was fed up with her so I had to block her from calling.

Just recently, she started calling from somebody else's phone with her bullshit. She ended up finding out about me and her sister. Alexus told me that she let it be known when they followed her in the mall. I wasn't mad at her for telling it because she would have found out eventually. I was more worried about Lex finding out that it happened since we've been together. The situation was fucked up, but it was too late for regrets. Like I told her, her sister could have turned me down so she was as much at fault as I was.

Sometimes I didn't understand how or why Cherika even wanted me. I did things that no married man should have ever done. She lowered her standards so many times just to please me, but it was never enough to keep me from wandering. Another woman had done something that she could never do and that was make me fall in love. That was something that I swore I would never do.

I loved Cherika, but I was never in love with her. I loved her for all the wrong reasons. She accepted things that Alexus or no other woman would ever put up with. She made me more of a priority than herself and my kids and I hated that. Cherika's self-esteem was low and that was unattractive to me.

Alexus had more confidence than women twice her age. That was one of the things that drew me to her. She made it known that she wanted me, but she didn't need me. She was demonstrating that now since I had been calling her phone nonstop for over two hours without getting an answer. I had a feeling that she was on some bullshit again. She was never home anymore and when I asked her anything about her whereabouts, she would blow up.

I promised her that I wasn't going to put my hands on her any more, but she was making it hard. I didn't want to think that somebody else was in the picture, but that's what all the signs pointed to. Jada probably knew everything that was going on, but I couldn't even be mad at her though. Her loyalty was to Alexus and not me. Knowing Jada, she probably encouraged her to mess around.

I was about to pick up my phone and call this chick that I met a few days ago. I needed something or someone to get my mind off of Alexus and our problems. Before I could dial her number, my phone started to ring. I got excited for a second, thinking it might be my baby. That was only until I saw Keanna's number flash across my screen. Out of all people in the world to call me, I couldn't believe it was her.

I hadn't talked to Keanna in a few months. I wasn't mad at her for doing the DNA test, even though I wish she had come to me first. I was pissed about how she played both sides when it came to Cherika and Alexus. It never crossed my mind that she was the one who put Cherika down on everything that went on with us. Especially since she was the one who brought us together in the first place. I guess that was her way of getting back at Cherika for dealing with Troy. I was still wondering how she found out about that in the first place. I know he didn't volunteer that information and Cherika would have died before she said anything. The only reason she told my family the truth was because she wanted their help in getting me back.

I looked down at my ringing phone that displayed Keanna's number for the sixth time in a row. Something was telling me to answer, but I let it go to voicemail once again. I wondered what could have been so serious that she would call me. After Cherika told me that she was the one who supplied her with all of her info, I cursed her ass out and told her I was done with her. One thing I hated was a snake. And she was the worst kind. She had me fooled and that was damn hard to do.

My phone started ringing again. This time, curiosity got the best of me and I decided to pick up to see what she wanted. I know it couldn't be anything wrong with the family because somebody else would be calling me too.

"Fuck is you blowing my phone up for!" I yelled into the receiver. "I told you I don't fuck with your snake ass any more." I could tell she was shocked at the way I answered because she paused for a minute before she spoke.

"I know I'm probably the last person you want to hear from, but it's kind of important," she said. I didn't know where she was, but the music was loud as hell in the background.

"What Keanna?" I said in an impatient tone.

"Um, are you and Alexus still together?" she asked hesitantly.

She had my undivided attention now. Keanna was messy as a mutha-fucka, but when she gave you some info, she was always right on the money. I had a feeling that she was about to tell me something that I didn't want or need to hear.

"Why you ask me that? What's up?" I asked.

"Well I'm at the grand opening for my friend's club and she's here," she replied. I knew there was more to the story, but I played along until she got to the point.

"Ok. I already know her and Jada went out. What's your point?" She was starting to piss me off with all this beating around the bush.

"Well Jada here too, but ole girl is in here with a dude."

My heart dropped when she said that last part. They always say females have intuition, but I sure as hell needed to know what it's called when a man had the same feelings. I knew something was up with her ass. The attitude change and constant complaining was a dead giveaway. It was cool though. I had something for her and that nigga she was with.

"What club y'all at Keanna?"

"It's a new club that just opened today. It's called Club Manhattan. It's on Manhattan Blvd. in Harvey," she replied. That was all I needed to know. I was on my way to shut that shit down.

"I'm on my way over there. Call me if she leaves," I told her before hanging up.

I jumped up from the sofa and went to my walk-in closet. It was hot outside, but I threw on some black sweat pants and a black hoodie. I wanted to be comfortable for whatever might pop off. I grabbed my keys and my gun from my dresser drawer and prepared to head out. I stopped in my tracks when I heard coughing coming from the other bedroom.

Damn! I was so busy rushing out of here to go see about Alexus, I almost left my kids in the house alone. I went into the bedroom to check on them and they were all still asleep. I hated to do it, but I had to wake them up. There was no way they could stay in here by themselves. I would just have to bring them home before I went anywhere. It was going to delay me a few minutes, but it had to be done.

"Where we going, Daddy?" My daughter asked me sleepily.

"I'm bringing y'all home. I have to go handle something right quick. I'll come get y'all again later on," I replied.

"Where's Alexus?" she asked.

"She's not here. I'm about to go get her now." I picked Drew up, while the rest of them followed me out to the car. I called Cherika to let her know that we were on our way.

"Hello," she answered on the first ring.

"Yeah, open the door. I'm about to bring them home," I told her. I used to have a key to Cherika's house until Alexus found out about it. She had a fit and I ended up throwing the damn thing away. I was getting mad all over again when I thought about her. I made changes to my life to make her happy, but she still wanted to fuck over me.

"Why, what's wrong?" Cherika asked shaking me from my thoughts.

"Nothing is wrong. I have to handle something and they can't be inside by themselves," I replied. I knew she was about to start bitching and I was absolutely right.

"Dre, it's almost two in the morning. What could you possibly have to handle at this hour?" she asked. "What your bitch don't want your children at y'all house or something?" I knew that was coming, but I really wasn't in the mood for it right now.

"you can miss me with the bullshit, just open the door. I'm on my way," I said disconnecting the call. I was already pissed off and I hoped and prayed that she didn't make it worse. She had a bad habit of popping off at the wrong time.

I pulled up to Cherika's house and saw her standing on the porch with her hands on her hips. I could tell that she wanted some drama, but I wasn't about to give it to her. I got out of the car, picked Drew up and proceeded to bring him into the house, with my other kids following close behind. I started walking up the stairs to put them back to bed when Cherika started with the questions.

"Where you going that's so important that you had to wake them up at this time of the morning?" she asked in her usual ghetto tone.

"Mind your fucking business," was all I said as I walked past her. I went to put Drew in her bed since he was still scared to sleep alone.

"He's going to get Alexus," my daughter said from behind us.

I couldn't get mad that she said it, especially since she was only repeating what I had told her. Cherika went crazy when she heard that.

"So you mean to tell me you got my kids out here at two in the fucking morning so you can run behind that stank bitch!" she yelled.

I didn't even answer her. She was trying to piss me off, but little did she know somebody had already beaten her to it. My phone started ringing and again, I assumed it was Alexus calling so I picked up without even looking at the screen.

"Yeah!" I yelled into my phone.

"Man where you at?" Eric said sounding upset.

"I just dropped my kids off home. Why, what's up?" I replied.

I listened as he told me about seeing Alexus with some nigga at the same club that Keanna told me about. He ended up having words with him before they left. To say I was heated was an understatement. She was running around with another nigga like I didn't exist. The shit was embarrassing enough, but for my people to call and tell me about it was a slap to my face.

"Yeah I heard. Keanna told me that y'all was on Manhattan, but where at on Manhattan?" I asked my brother.

Once he gave me the information I needed, I hung up and told him that I was on my way.

"Nigga you a sad ass excuse for a man. You're choosing that hoe over your children now!" Cherika screamed.

I continued to ignore her. I was just about to leave out of the room when she jumped in front of the door blocking it so I couldn't go.

"Move Cherika. I'm not in the mood for your foolishness," I said in a calm voice.

"Fuck that!" she yelled pushing me backwards.

"I'm tired of you putting everybody else before us." This girl was crazy for real.

"Who is us?" I yelled back at her.

"What part of we're not together don't you understand? And you better keep your fucking hands off of me."

I had a cake baking for that ass and I couldn't wait until it was done. She was about to get an eye opener any day now.

"What did I do so wrong to you? I did any and everything you wanted. I did things that I didn't even want to do for you," she cried.

Her tears didn't move me then and they damn sure didn't move me now. She did what she did because she wanted to.

"Look, I don't have time for this pity party you throwing yourself. I got moves to make," I said as I tried to walk past her.

I was almost out of the bedroom door when that crazy bitch threw an ashtray and hit me in the back of my head. I was seeing stars for a few seconds and I felt a little light headed. I touched the back of my head where she hit me and looked at the dark red blood that covered my hand. She ran in the bathroom and tried to lock the door, but I was too quick for her.

I blocked the door with my foot and grabbed her by the back of her shirt. She immediately started kicking and screaming, but that still didn't stop me. I picked her up and slammed her to the floor before hitting her with a closed fist.

"Help me, somebody help me!" she screamed to the top of her lungs.

I didn't have an ounce of sympathy for her. This all could have been avoided if she would have let me leave when I wanted to. She managed to grab a hold of one of my legs, causing me to fall. When I fell, she was able to crawl to the nightstand and grab the mace that she always kept there. There was no way in hell that was about to go down.

I jumped up before she was able to position it in my direction. I grabbed her wrist and twisted it until she dropped the can on the floor. I kicked it away from her as I held her hands to her side.

"Cherika, chill! I'm trying not to knock your ass out!" I yelled out of breath. This was the reason why I didn't come over here too often.

"Let me go!" she cried. "Nigga, you punched me in my face!"

She was acting like she didn't just bust my head open with a damn ashtray. I did feel bad, but she started the shit.

"I'm about to let you go, but you better not try to hit me anymore," I told her.

She didn't respond so I let her go and walked to the door. I looked back and saw her curled up on the floor crying. I hated to leave her in the position she was in, but I had more important moves to make.

I jumped in my truck and sped off towards the bridge. Alexus was about to see a side of me that she never knew existed.

My mind briefly drifted back to Cherika. I had done some major damage to her self-esteem and it was going to be a challenge for another man to restore it. If I never doubted anything in life, it wasn't her love for me. I knew I had her heart, but it wasn't my heart's desire. Yet, the one who had my heart wanted to give hers to someone else. It was true that karma was a bitch who had everybody's name and address. It hurt like hell to know that she was paying me a visit right now.

I came to a stop at a red light five minutes away from my destination. I was so caught up in my thoughts that I didn't see the police car behind me. When the light turned green, I pressed on the gas and continued to my destination. Unfortunately I didn't get very far before he turned his sirens on and started tailing me. I tried switching lanes like I normally did hoping he would pass me by, but he switched lanes right along with me. Having no other choice, I pulled over into the gas station and waited for him to come to me. He sat in his car until two other cruisers pulled up, then he got out. I didn't know what the hell he stopped me for, but I was about to find out.

"Step out of the car for me please," the officer said as he approached my car.

"What's the problem sir?" I asked in my most sincere voice.

"Just step out of the car please," he repeated in a no nonsense tone. I wasn't trying to give them no reason to kill my black ass so I did as I was told.

"We got a call about a domestic dispute and your license plate matches the one given to us by the victim," another officer said. I couldn't believe this shit. That bitch Cherika sent the law after me. Cherika and I fought like wild animals during the entire course of our relationship, but not one time did she ever get the police involved.

"Turn around and put your hands on the car," the officer told me. I did as I was told, while the officer began to frisk me.

"You got anything on your person or in your car that we should know about?"

"Naw, I'm clean."

"I got something here," the officer who searched my car yelled.

I knew I was fucked when I saw him come up with my gun. The gun was clean and the paperwork was in Erica's name. The problem was that I was on probation so I shouldn't have had it in the first place. There was no doubt in my mind that I was about to be taking a ride. I was handcuffed and put in the back of the car. My phone was ringing off the hook, but that was the least of my problems.

"Excuse me sir. Can I just call my brother and let him know what's going on so he can come get my car and my wallet, please?" I asked the only black officer out there.

I was hoping he would have some kind of compassion and help me out. He didn't answer at first, but after a while, he came over to the car with my phone in his hand.

"I can't uncuff you, but give me the number and I'll let you talk on the speaker phone," he said.

I was grateful for that much because he didn't have to do it. He dialed Eric's number for me and he picked up on the first ring. He told me that he and Keanna weren't far from where I was and he would be there shortly. I thought about Alexus once again. I guess ole boy won this round since there was nothing that I could do. I prepared my mind to go back to a place where I swore I would never go again; jail.

Chapter 23
CHERIKA

"Hello," I said answering my phone. I really didn't feel like talking to anyone, but I know my mama would be on her way over if I didn't answer.

"Hey baby. How you feeling?" she asked in her usual concerned tone. I felt like shit, but I would never tell her that.

"I'm good ma. I'm feeling much better," I lied.

"You don't sound like you're feeling better. Have you eaten anything?" she said. My mother was the one person who could see right through me without even trying.

"I haven't eaten yet, but I'm probably going to order a pizza," I replied.

That was another lie. I hadn't eaten anything for the past two days and I didn't have any plans on eating today. Once again, I was depressed and all alone. My mom and my sister's had my kids because I was in no shape to care for them. They didn't want them to see me in the condition I was in.

"Cherika, you need to come over here with me and your sisters. You should be with family at a time like this. Or we can come and spend a few days over there if you want us to. I know these babies miss you and their house," My mama said.

I missed my kids to death, but it wasn't much that I could do for them right now. I stayed in the bed or on the sofa most of the day. It wouldn't be fair to them to be inside all day while I moped around feeling sorry for myself.

"It's quiet in there. where are my kids?" I asked changing the subject.

"Charde took them to the store," she replied.

We both held the phone without speaking for a while. I know my mother was only trying to help, but I had to figure my own way out of the mess that I created.

"Well, I'll let you go, but if you change your mind about coming over, just give me a call," she said before disconnecting our call.

I was so happy that she didn't push the issue like she would normally do. I just wanted to be left alone with my thoughts.

It had been three days since Dre got locked up. I only wanted to teach him a lesson for putting his hands on me, but I never intended to press charges against him. It never dawned on me that he might have had a gun on him. Now he was being held for a probation violation. That was never a part of the plan and I regretted the decision I made to get the police involved. I was just so hurt when Dre left that night and my emotions were all over the place.

I was hurt that he always chose Alexus over me and our kids. I was the one who held him down each and every time he went to jail. I was the one who he gave birth to his kids. And I was the only one whose hand he took in marriage. Even after all of that, Alexus always seemed to reap the benefits of my hard labor. It was fucked up that he could leave me for cheating on him when she was doing the exact same thing. I saw it with my own eyes, but he didn't care. No matter how much I tried to deny it, she truly had my husband's heart and the pain was too much to bear. As crazy as it sounded, I was happy that he was in jail for one reason only; Alexus couldn't have him either.

Dre's entire family was mad with me for sending him to jail. I really wanted to talk to him so that I could apologize for what I did and let him know that I would be dropping the charges. I tried calling Eric and his sisters, but none of them wanted to talk to me. His mother told me to give everybody some time to come around, but I doubted that they ever would. It was no surprise that his dad flat out told me not to call his phone again. I was never one of his favorites anyway.

They never even tried to consider how I might be feeling at the moment. I'd been bending over backwards to please Dre since day one and everything I did was to make him happy. I knew that he wasn't the marrying type, but none of that mattered to me. I thought if I did everything right he would change.

When I saw that he was getting bored with our marriage, I offered to let him bring other women into our bedroom. That was the beginning of the end of our marriage. Soon after that is when Alexus came into the picture and the rest was history.

I got up from my spot on the sofa and decided to go through the mail that was piling up on the floor while I waited. I was hoping that Dre would at least write to let me know what was going on with him, but he never did. I caught a glimpse of my reflection in the mirror when I stood up and I was a complete mess. My hair was matted on top of my head like a beehive and my right eye was black and slightly swollen from when Dre hit me the other day. I shuffled through some junk mail until I came upon a letter that was addressed to both me and Dre.

I jumped when I heard the timer go off in my bathroom. I was nervous, but I was ready to get it over with. I walked into the bathroom, opening the letter that I had just discovered in my mail. I dropped down to the floor in tears as I read the contents of the letter. Dre had made a fool of me once again. Here I was with a positive pregnancy test in one hand and divorce papers in the other.

To Be Continued

ACKNOWLEDGEMENTS

First, I want to give thanks to the almighty God. I have been blessed with many talents and I am so very thankful for them all.

To my children, Lil Terrence and Kiara, both of you are the reason I work as hard as I do on and off the clock. The love I have for you cannot be measured.

To my mother, Rhette Parker, words will never be able to describe how thankful and blessed I am to have you in my life. I can never remember a time that you were not there for your kids and grandkids and I love you to death for it.

My father, the late Lionel Parker, I wish you were here to see all that your girls have accomplished. Your memories will be with us forverer.

To my sisters, Racquel, Lynell and Trina Parker, who keep me laughing no matter how my day is going. I love y'all so much even if I don't say it every day.

My grandpa, Jeff Stirgus, who has been like a second father to me since I can remember, we are truly blessed to have you in our lives.

My aunts, Susan and Serita, who are the best aunts a girl could ever ask for.

My cousins, Aunts, Uncles and Friends (It's too many of them to name) who I don't see every day, but it feels like it when we get together. Your support means the world to me and I cherish it.

My co-workers/friends, Trina J., Mattie, Kelly, Latrice, Danielle, TaGermanie, Roderick, Amy and Michelle, who were there encouraging me every step of the way. The support from you all was so amazing and I can't thank you enough.

A special thanks to my girl, QuoVadis (Quo), who wore so many hats, it was hard to keep up. I appreciate all the time and energy you put into being a proofreader, photographer, make-up artist, Etc., even if you did want to kill me at times ☺

A special thanks to Torica Tymes (who is a sweetheart by the way) for believing in me enough to welcome me into the Write House Family.

To Cole Hart who answered any questions I had and provided some much needed advice and feedback. To Tiece and the entire Write House/TBRS Family for making me feel welcomed from day one.

A special shout out goes to the very talented stylists at So Xclusive Hair Studio.

Last, but not least, a big thank you to everyone who purchased a copy of this book. Your support is greatly appreciated and I hope you enjoy.

I hope I didn't forget anyone, but if I did, charge to my head and not my heart because it was not intentional.